MW00579892

ROSALIE'S

CROSSING

R. A. McCAIN

R .   A .   M c C A I N

Copyright 2019 © by Ryan Andrew McCain

All rights reserved.

This book or any portion thereof may not be reproduced or used in
any manner whatsoever without the express written permission of
the publisher except for use of brief quotations in a book review.

Printed in the United States of America

ISBN: 978-1-7331878-0-0

Barn Burner Publishing, LLC

10203 Broken Trace Ct

Humble, TX 77338

TABLE OF CONTENTS

R . A . McCAIN

This book is dedicated to my wife.
You are proof that dreams come true.

CHAPTER ONE
THE CARPET LADIES

Houston, Texas.

Amidsize, white utility van exits the I-10 freeway just outside of Baytown and pulls off onto a narrow dirt road. The road bends around a large mound of earth that was bulldozed into a makeshift wall. The van stops after a hundred yards, and parks in a secluded field. The area is densely populated with scrub brush and tall weeds. Two men slowly exit the vehicle, deeply engrossed in conversation.

Rodrigo, who exits the passenger side, is a tall, lean man with a very muscular build. "Besides, I like white women better," he says as he walks to the back of the van. Slowly and powerfully, he hits the side of the van with a hammer-fist, landing a blow with each step he takes.

Alger exits the driver's side. Alger is a short, fat man wearing a high-end Hawaiian shirt and cargo pants. "You need to stay away from those white bitches. When they get upset, they try to get you deported. You need to get yourself a good Mexican woman."

"What, like these *putas*?" asks Rodrigo as he opens the back of the van. The eight dirty and terrified Mexican women inside avoid his gaze, all staring meekly at the floor. Speaking in Spanish, Rodrigo thrusts his chin at one of the women and says, "You, fat girl, go lay the carpets down."

Alger removes his cowboy hat to wipe the sweat from his brow. "Hey!" he says, squinting against the sun and pointing his hat in the girl's direction. "Not too close, those guys don't need to be all up on each other."

The chubby girl does as she is told. She begins by grabbing one of the eight rolled-up pieces of old carpet, six- by four-foot scraps, and unrolls it on a somewhat flat area in the brush. She repeats the process with the remaining rolls of carpet as Rodrigo and Alger resume their conversation in English.

"Look at you, wearing your Tommy Bahama. You're telling me that you don't go for white women?" Rodrigo raises his eyebrows, feigning disbelief.

"Fuck no, *mano*, I just like the way my man Tommy makes these shirts breathe."

Rodrigo laughs. "I left Mexico to get away from Mexico, *mano*. What's less Mexican than a white bitch?"

Alger simply shakes his head, then peeks around the side of the van toward the dirt wall. Rodrigo follows suit; they see nothing, and return to their conversation.

The chubby girl finishes laying the last carpet down. As she returns to the van, Rodrigo begins to chide her on. "Hey, *Gorda*, how come you're still so fat? You got one of those carpet fucks sneaking you food?"

She tries to walk by, respectfully ignoring him, but Rodrigo grabs her by the arm, forcing her to face him. "Do they sneak you French fries, fat girl? Lift up your skirt!" Her shoulders slump as she lifts her skirt, revealing an extremely hairy and unclean vagina, abused and sore from the marathon sex sessions she is forced to endure. "Ah ha! You're smuggling Mole in your *chones*, you dirty bitch," says Rodrigo, cackling as he splashes water from the mouth of his water bottle at her vagina. "You need to clean that better if you expect these guys to pay for it."

"They'll still pay," says Alger as he laughs. The woman lowers her skirt, hunching into herself, and tries to re-enter the van. "What the fuck are you doing?" Alger sneers in Spanish. "All you dummies, get out on your carpet!"

One of the girls near the front of the van asks, "Can't we stay in the shade?"

Rodrigo mistakes a young girl named Rosalie, sitting near the middle of the van, as being the one who asked the question. Furious, he reaches in and grabs her by the hair, and uses his grip to yank her out and throw her into the dirt. "What? Are you hot? Are you thirsty?" Rodrigo barks. Rosalie remains silent as Rodrigo weaves his fingers more tightly through her hair, cradling the back of her head. He suddenly tightens his grip into a fist, and she winces as her hair threatens to come out at the root; he now controls every movement of her head. "Open your mouth and stick out your tongue."

She does as she's told. He begins to trickle water over every part of her face, save for her mouth, without moving the bottle; rather, he tilts and skews her head under the light stream of water.

After the bottle is empty, and all that has reached her mouth was what happened to drip from the tip of her nose, he leans in close and whispers, "That's all the water you get today."

Alger notices a truck full of men in the distance. "All right, ladies, go pick a piece of carpet and lay down," he says in Spanish. As the women exit the van, Alger hands each of them an egg timer from a plastic bag. "Ten minutes only."

Rodrigo releases his grip on Rosalie and nods for her to collect an egg timer. As Rosalie walks toward Alger, one of the other new girls asks about the egg timer. *"Que es esto?"*

Alger grabs one and shows both the young girl and Rosalie how to use the device. "Turn this knob until it reaches ten, then let go. The wheel will begin to turn. Once ten minutes has passed, the timer will ring. That is when the man will get off you. Then you turn it back to ten when the next man gets on top of you. You keep doing this until we put you back in the van. If the man finishes before ten minutes is done, you twist this back to zero so we hear a ring and make him leave. Ten minutes only."

Focusing on Rosalie, he adds, "I'd be surprised if they get to ten minutes with you, sweetheart." He lightly caresses Rosalie's face. "Understand?" he asks with a sudden sharpness as he gives Rosalie's face a light, yet firm slap across her cheek. Both women nod their heads. "Well, go the fuck away, then."

The women make their way over to claim the two remaining pieces of carpet.

A line of men has quickly formed near the rear of the van, and more vehicles continue to arrive. Most know the drill. Some are new guys, who have heard about this place by word of mouth in the fields that they work. *"Cuanto cuesta?"* asks the first man.

Alger replies, "I recognize you. You know how much it costs." The man quickly produces a ten-dollar bill and gives it to Alger. "Don't fuck with me again," he says as he grants passage.

The man briskly walks into the open-air sex market and begins to window shop amongst the women. Most are lying on their backs with their forearms and hands shielding their eyes from the sun. He stops when he sees Rosalie, who is lying on her back, clutching the sides of her skirt in a hopeless effort to keep it from blowing up in the slight breeze. The man has found his prize.

He quickly drops to his knees and begins to undo his belt. Once he has his pants unbuttoned and zipper drawn down, he easily spreads Rosalie's legs; even if she would dare to put up a fight, she is too weak, and they both know it. He begins to thrust into her, and in the haste of the whole encounter—and the shock of the searing, sandpaper-like pain of being filled when it is not welcome—she forgets to start the egg timer.

After what feels like an eternity to her, he says, *"Quiero ese culito."* His breath is hot and moist against her neck, and she thinks of screaming, but knows what that will bring. Too quickly for her to process, he has flipped her over on her stomach, and pinned her hands to her sides. "Stick your ass out," he commands.

Face-down, she squeezes her eyes shut against the blinding pain she knows will come next.

Just as he is about to penetrate her, Rodrigo grabs the man by his hair. As he pulls the man's head back, Rodrigo places the edge of his knife against the man's throat. "Don't do that. You didn't pay for that," he hisses.

Rosalie holds her breath.

"Cuanto cuesta?" asks the man, a tremor in his voice.

"Viente dolares mas," replies Rodrigo. He reaches down into the man's pocket, his blade still firmly held against the man's jugular. He removes a wad of cash, a total of sixteen dollars, then asks the man if that is all he has. The man replies, "Si."

Rosalie releases her pent-up breath; at least she has avoided that, for now.

Rodrigo takes the blade away from the man's throat and pockets the money. As he un-straddles the man, he places his knife back in its sheath and straightens to standing, but before he walks away, he swiftly and powerfully kicks the man in his right side. "Next time, bring enough money for what you want," shouts Rodrigo for the whole field to hear.

The commotion has gotten Alger's attention. He stops his collections to take account of the situation as he grips his handgun, still in its holster. As Alger sees Rodrigo continuing his rounds, checking in on the girls, he resumes his sales. "Okay, *mano*. It's ten dollars for the pussy, twenty dollars for the ass. You only get ten minutes. What do you want?"

"Pussy, please. Do you have condoms?" asks the man as he hands over ten dollars.

"If you want condoms, bring them yourself. I'm not your mama," Alger replies as he points the man toward an available woman.

Rosalie's hands are finally free as the man on top of her finishes and begins to stand up. She can hear him walking away and an uncontrollable sob bursts forth from deep in her chest. Quickly, she struggles to regain her composure; she remembers what one of the other girls said to her in the van: "Don't cry. They will cut your face if you cry." As she fights back the tears, another man mounts her and pushes her head down, the unexpected assault causing her breath to rush out in a high-pitched shriek. With her face now being smothered in the carpet as the man gyrates on top of her, steadily increasing to a rapid pace, she silently prays to God to save her. The words are heard only in her head.

Eight women, each living out her own personal hell on a scrap of carpet. From the woman being choked until the man climaxes, to the woman with a piercing rock digging into her back as he thrusts his whole bodyweight into her, each woman prays for some small miracle to make her life a little less terrible.

Many hours pass, and the sun begins to set behind a now cloudy sky. Only after the last customer leaves satisfied, and no hope of another patron can be seen in the distance, does Rodrigo come to collect the women and order them back into the van. They all rise. Some slowly, some more injured than others. They are ordered to roll up their carpets and pile into the van. As the last girl practically falls into the van, Rodrigo slams the door shut.

"How much today?" asks Rodrigo, turning to Alger.

Alger grins. "$2,120."

"Wow, it's been a while since we broke two thousand...plus, we got an extra sixteen dollars for dinner."

The men rejoice as they enter the van. Alger throws it into gear and they drive off toward the highway.

The women in the back all stare forward, almost in a daze, each not quite looking at the woman across from her, but staring through her. All of them trying not to relive the day's events in their heads; trying not to feel the pain and humiliation that weigh them down. The forty-minute commute and dollar-menu hamburgers are just a brief respite for these women. Their evening will be spent sleeping in a small shed behind a house in the suburbs, restrained by a padlock on the outside and a severe beating if they call out for help. Eight women, sleeping huddled together with just a small bucket for a bathroom.

As the sun finally sets, the back of the van becomes almost pitch black. Rosalie welcomes the darkness, so no one will see the tears she can no longer hold back. To no one in particular, she asks, "Is this all there is?"

Another voice replies, "Don't worry...tomorrow is Sunday. We'll get to shower."

The women collectively sigh, and their night ends as they are shuffled from van to shed, where they fall fast asleep.

CHAPTER TWO
THE ICE AGENTS

Houston, Texas.

The men and women of Immigration and Customs Enforcement come from all walks of life. Gabriel Granado, a man of half Puerto Rican, half Cuban descent, served five years in the United States Navy. As a Master at Arms aboard the USS Abraham Lincoln, he buckled down and earned a bachelor's degree in Criminal Justice. Having faithfully served his country, he was quickly hired as an ICE agent upon leaving active duty. Standing five feet, seven inches tall, he doesn't have the typical demeanor found in shorter men. He isn't self-conscious, nor is he overconfident. He is good at his job, and is often looked to for advice and guidance by his fellow agents.

"You guys seen this shit? This fucker is gonna get himself killed!" says Gabriel, intently watching his computer monitor. Playing on the screen is a video of a man hounding other men as they enter Asian bath houses.

"Sir, excuse me, sir. How do you think your wife would feel if she knew you were here getting your pipe cleaned by a sex slave?" the protagonist of the video asks. The man being pestered doesn't reply and attempts to block the camera from recording his face as he gets into his car.

The protagonist, known as the "Video Vigilante," gets into his own car and performs a monologue about how vile and evil these "sex prisons" are. He sees another man exit the brothel and decides to follow him. "We're just gonna follow this little sinner and see where he lives. Let's see how his family likes having their story plastered all over the internet. To all you WHORE MONGERS out there, be advised, I will record you, and I will FUCK your whole world up! That is, unless you stop frequenting these whore houses, so they will be forced to move out of our neighborhoods."

Gabriel leans back and folds his hands behind his head. "We might have to put the HPD on this guy. The cartels are gonna fucking kill this dude."

"What are you talking about?" Agent Louis Bennett asks, craning his neck in an attempt to see what Gabriel is looking at.

Gabriel gives him a sidelong glance, curling his lip at the newbie. "Jesus fucking Christ, new guy, do you pay attention to anything? This Video Vigilante guy that's been posting shit all over YouTube about Asian fuck fuck houses. He's been videotaping johns going in and out of these places, putting their license plate numbers on his blog. He caught Judge McCoy the other day and the fucker had to resign. Don't you read the FLASH reports? Or do you sit there and fart into your hand all fucking day?"

Louis has only been with the Agency a few months, just recently finished his initial training. He is young, and at twenty-four years of age, has virtually no experience in the area of law enforcement.

"Alright, alright, that's enough. Stop fucking with the new guy," says Special Agent in Charge David Uribe, as he exits his private office. Uribe has been working as a federal agent in various capacities for almost thirty years. He did time as a DEA agent working deep cover along the border in San Diego during the early 80s. Only after a cartel put a bounty on his head did he transfer to a much safer posting in Immigration and Customs Enforcement.

"Nah, nah, fuck that shit. It's his constitutionally protected right to fuck with the new guy," Agent Teresa Velazquez says, barely raising her eyes from the computer she's sitting at across from Gabriel. Teresa is what most men would characterize as a sexy tomboy. She stands a commanding five feet, zero inches tall and has a personality the size of a mountain. She is a third-generation American, but still feels as though she has strong ties to Mexico. Growing up, her grandparents would tell her about their trials and tribulations crossing the border. Theirs is the American success story of immigrating to the United States and finding happiness.

"Yeah, this is still America, right?" Gabriel grins at Uribe, and the man rolls his eyes. Turning back to Teresa, Gabriel adds, "And I don't need you defending me; I'm a big boy."

"Fine. I was just trying to support my teammate. Shit, that's why these fuckers are winning. It's because we can't even team up to fuck with a new guy, let alone bring down a sophisticated network of drug and pussy smuggling." She raises her eyes to look him up and down briefly, then adds, "Oh, and you are a big boy...getting bigger every day. Put down the donut—that gut is probably why your wife don't want to fuck you no more. When was the last time you saw your dick, anyway?"

Puffing up his chest, Gabriel says, "I don't need to see it, your mom looked at it the other day and said it looked just fine."

Teresa throws her head back and laughs. When she's regained herself, she asks, "How is mom doing?"

"She's good. She wishes you'd call more," says Gabriel. Teresa just shakes her head, a smile still playing at her lips, and goes back to her work. Gabriel resumes the paused video and fast forwards to a point where the Vigilante confronts a man in his own driveway.

The man's wife and children are in the front yard, confusion written on their faces. "Ma'am...ma'am. Do you know where your husband just came from?" The man tells the vigilante to shut up. "No, I won't fucking shut up," he sneers at the man. Turning back to the wife, he tells her, "He was with a whore in Upper Kirby. I have video evidence and pictures. They'll be on my website, River Oaks Vigilante dot com. Don't be a sucker. Get out of this hell, before he takes you down with him." The video ends with the Vigilante being pushed off the lawn by the man in question.

Teresa, who was listening though she couldn't see the screen, says, "You're right, that fucker is gonna die, but HPD won't put surveillance on him. They're too busy dealing with gangs in the fifth ward."

"Alright Bennett, you being new, maybe you can give us a fresh take on how to bring down this human trafficking problem," says Uribe.

At first, Agent Bennett looks like a deer in the headlights, then as though a light has clicked on in his head. "Raids! Keep hitting them over and over, and soon enough they'll have to go out of business."

The trio of experienced agents look at one another, and Uribe rolls his eyes again—as if no one had ever thought of that. Teresa is the one to rip him a new one: "You forgot one thing, fucktard— that's fucking stupid and it won't work. Do you know how fucking expensive raids are? Ohh, and what about legal proceedings for making false entries into licensed businesses, with no real probable cause? The only way to win is to take away the demand. And that, my friend, would require castrating every man in the United States." She shoots him a piercing look. "A task that I'm more than up for."

"Teresa, quit scaring the new guy," Uribe grumbles, but adds, "Louis, that was fucking dumb. Get your head in the game."

"Ironically enough, my unseasoned friend, we have a raid planned for later today," says Gabriel.

The poor kid just looks confused now. "Really?"

"Yup, with the DEA. Apparently, they tracked some drug activity to a known brothel in Humble. We're gonna go in for the assist."

Uribe nods and his face grows serious as he folds his arms across his chest. "The three of you will meet at the mount site, in the parking lot of that barbeque joint on the corner of FM 1960 and

HWY 59, at 1300. DEA Special Agent Valdez is running point on this and has tactical command. We'll take custody of and process any illegals found in the house; the DEA will take care of the rest. Got it?"

"Got it, boss," Gabriel says, and the other agents nod.

"Okay." Uribe claps his hands and rubs them together. "Stay safe." The Special Agent in Charge turns away from his agents, retiring to his office.

"Looks like we're gonna get to break your raid cherry new guy," says Teresa, a manic sort of gleam in her eye.

Gabriel winces, bringing a hand to his forehead. Then, slowly enunciating every word, says, "*Pop*...it's fucking *pop your cherry*, Teresa! Jesus—you had one at one point, and don't even know how to say it right!"

"Alright, alright." She holds up her hands in surrender, then gathers her stuff. As she puts on her jacket, she quips, "Don't bring that negativity to the raid later, that shit messes with my energy, *papi*."

The three agents walk toward the office exit and depart for the armory.

CHAPTER THREE
COCHOAPA EL GRANDE

Cochoapa el Grande, Guerrero, Mexico.

With a population of 2,600 and zero influence in the government, the town is at the mercy of Los Guerreros Del Selva, or The Jungle Warriors, the most powerful cartel in the territory of Guerrero. With the tortures and injustices at the hands of the military still burning painfully in the memories of the townsfolk, they find little difference in the changing of the guard.

For years, the soldiers sent to police the town spent their days raping the women and pillaging the farms for food. Only recently did the newly elected President institute his crusade against hunger. A community kitchen was erected, and the military assets in the town were re-deployed to other parts of the country in greater need of "help." For a short while, the citizens rejoiced in the peace and tranquility of a "lawless" state.

Rosalie Bolanos is one of the area's native children. An only child, sixteen years of age, she is still a virgin. A rarity for a girl in a region known for its crimes against women. She's spent most of her life avoiding rape through the shelter and ingenuity of her parents. A blessing or a curse, her breathtaking beauty has made this more difficult over the years. Slight in frame, which is normal for the petite women in her family, it's accentuated by the family's lack of food and adequate shelter; her parents are simple farmers, with a small plot of land and only a cramped shack to call home.

Her father, Ronaldo, knows too well the horrors that evil men are capable of. When he was a child, his older brother was kidnapped by a group of men and held for ransom. With no money or resources at their disposal, his family attempted to plead with the kidnappers, but their appeal fell on deaf ears. After three weeks of what seemed to be empty threats, the gangsters were finally forced to prove their resolve: A photograph of his headless corpse was left on the family doorstep. The body was never found, and the devastated family had no recourse. In the territory of Guerrero, lawmen can be just as corrupt as the criminals...more so, in some cases.

"Papa, why does the kitchen never have any food?" young Rosalie asks her father.

"We don't need their food. We can grow our own now. What we grow, we can keep. No more giving it to the captains and privates," her father promises.

Rosalie smiles, turning her cheek into her father's hand as he brushes a strand of hair back behind her ear.

"Rosalie, come here, my love," María, her mother, calls to her from that small shack of a house. When Rosalie runs over, she chastises the girl. "Why are you not wearing your scarf?"

"Papa said I don't need to cover up anymore, now that the soldiers are gone," replies young Rosalie, an innocent naiveté creasing her brow as she looks at her mother.

"That may be, but there are always men that will want to take from a pretty girl." Her mother nudges her, and Rosalie goes to her bed and picks up the amber colored scarf. She delicately wraps it around her head, covering all but her eyes.

As Rosalie goes outside to rejoin her father in his chores, a red truck pulls up to the house. From the truck, two men emerge. Four other men remain seated in the bed of the pickup, clutching assault rifles as they glare at Ronaldo, their chins out.

"Hola, senor. How are you doing today?" The younger of the two men, Rito, oozes with faux charm. Rito is in his mid-twenties and has a wonderfully thick beard. The other man is Juan. He's a slender man with a clean-shaven face and thinning hair. As Rito stares at Ronaldo, awaiting his reply, Juan approaches the doorway to the house and looks inside.

Ronaldo's mouth has gone dry, his palms sweaty. Still, he tries not to convey the anxiety washing through his body when he speaks. "We are fine. Is there anything I can help you with?"

Unable to control the impulse to protect his family, Ronaldo walks toward Juan in an effort to stop his advance into the house. Rito intercedes, cutting off Ronaldo's approach, and says, "We're going to be running things around here now. We just want to get to know our people."

Ronaldo scoffs indignantly at the man's words, fury now pulsing in tandem with his fear. He spits, "We are not your people. We don't know you." As Ronaldo brushes past Rito, completely disregarding Rito's presence in his path, Rito lashes out suddenly, kicking in the back of one of Ronaldo's knees.

Ronaldo's body crumples as his knee gives out. Just as Ronaldo lands hard in the dirt, Rito slams his boot into Ronaldo's stomach. "You are OUR people because I say that you are OUR people!" Rito barks, each word punctuated by another blow, as he towers over Ronaldo. The four other men swiftly jump off of the truck and take positions surrounding the area. "A man with a family shouldn't be so quick to say 'No' to new friends," Rito says, calmer now—Rosalie has caught his eye.

She trembles as the man walks over to her, a sick grin splitting his face. Already, she feels unclean beneath his gaze. He caresses her cheek through the amber fabric, settling his fingers beneath her chin to tilt her head up, and she casts her eyes to the ground defiantly.

"It's not very sunny today, *amore*. Why are you wearing a scarf like that?"

Ronaldo, still doubled over and wheezing, manages to say, "She is sick. She has tuberculosis."

Juan centers himself in the doorway and removes a large knife from the sheath on his belt. His presence blocks María's attempt to give aid.

"Been smoking too much tobacco, *amore*? I haven't heard you cough. Maybe this mountain air has cured you." Rito laughs at his own joke, then swiftly grabs the scarf and yanks it clean from the girl's head. "It's a miracle! Instead of a disease-infested little *puta*, we have a beautiful angel." Rito turns his eyes on Ronaldo, scowling. "I think you were trying to hide her from us. What do you think? That we are monsters? That we were going to rape your little angel?"

Ronaldo remains silent—there is no right answer. Rito squats down and looks Ronaldo directly in his eyes. "You know, *mano*, right now, looking into your eyes...I see that you don't want to be a part of us. You're like a dog backed into a corner. One thing that I've learned in my life, is that you gotta put down that kind of dog." For a long moment, Rito searches Ronaldo's eyes, only serving to delay what Ronaldo knows is coming for him.

Suddenly, Rito stands and nods to one of the men wielding a rifle, and just like that, it's over. A single round fired into the back of Ronaldo's head.

María begins to scream, and Juan grabs her by the throat, holding her up against the frame of the doorway. As Juan presses the flat side of his knife against her cheek, he calmly says, "Your husband is gone. Think about your daughter. We won't hurt her if you do what we want."

María attempts to control herself but can't fight back the tears welling up in her eyes. Her whole body trembles. Rosalie, however, remains silent. Not even the faintest whimper escapes her; she is frozen still with fear.

"Damn...you're a tough little girl, aren't you? You didn't even flinch when you heard the gun," says Rito, eyeing her with a strange expression as he slowly walks back to her. "That's good," he whispers, leaning in close to her ear, "you're gonna need to be tough where you're going."

He quickly turns and walks toward María. Getting in her face, he spells it out for her: "Mama, listen to me! We are taking your little girl to the United States. She is going to work in one of our factories there. She'll be taken care of. The Americans like cheap labor that doesn't cause any problems. You are going to stay here and help with our drug operation. If you refuse...well..." Stuffing his hands in his pockets, he takes a casual stance, shrugging as if to say, *You may not like it, but this is how it is.* Then he pins her with a piercing stare. "Your daughter will be raped and beaten. We will bury her alive, but not before we burn her face with gasoline."

Wild-eyed, Juan's hand still around her throat, María does her best to nod, a slight, frantic motion but enough for Rito.

He swings back toward Rosalie. "And you, little girl. You will not cause us one bit of trouble. You will not make a sound while you belong to us, or I swear to God, we will slice your mother from her pussy to her chin and leave her for the ants to eat!" he threatens, motioning as though his finger is a knife, cleanly slicing María in one vertical swipe. "Do you understand?"

Rosalie quickly nods, her mouth still tightly shut; the only indication she is affected at all is the rapid rising and falling of her chest, her nostrils flaring.

Rito shows his satisfaction with a curt nod. "Go say goodbye to your mother," he says as he walks back toward the truck.

Rosalie and María, finally released from Juan's grip, run to each other. María gathers her daughter in her arms, holding her only child in a vice-like grip. The dam breaks and tears flow freely now, mother and daughter sobbing uncontrollably. After a moment, María sniffs and takes a deep breath. Into her daughter's hair, she says, "My angel, do whatever they say. Whenever you get to where you are going, find an older woman to look after you. Those factories are dangerous, and they won't care about you. Be safe and don't cause trouble. Eventually, you will be free."

Rosalie can't bring herself to move, her face buried deep in her mother's bosom. She clings to María for dear life. A fresh sob racks her frail body, and the force of it nearly overwhelms María again.

Breathing slowly through her nose so she won't lose her composure, María gently pushes Rosalie away. She removes a thin gold chain with a crucifix from around her neck, and as she puts it over her daughter's head, she says, "Be strong Rosalie. Take this, and you will always have me with you."

"That's enough! Time to leave!" Juan grabs Rosalie by the arm and pulls her toward the truck.

María seizes the final moments of opportunity to whisper into her daughter's ear, "Keep coughing, they won't want sex with you if they think you are sick," and then Rosalie is out of reach.

Juan opens the passenger side door and motions for Rosalie to get in. The young girl climbs in and sits in the middle, between Rito and Juan. As the truck speeds away, María clings to the hope that her daughter will be a simple factory worker. Despite her best efforts, the fear that Rosalie will be ravaged by random men every moment for the rest of her life creeps into María's thoughts as the truck goes behind a bend in the mountain road. It turns out of sight...never to be seen again. As María looks down at her husband's body, reality sets in—her world will never be the same. She collapses to the ground with shock, hollow-eyed, too overwhelmed to even cry.

CHAPTER FOUR
THE RAID

DEA Special Agent Jason Valdez sits in the driver's seat of a parked SUV. Valdez is a young man—seemingly too young to have the moniker "Special Agent." However young he may seem, he is one of the agency's best investigators.

Gabriel is in the passenger seat. Parked in a small strip mall, in front of a closed doughnut shop, they are observing a run-down house, half a block down the street.

Bored and becoming antsy, Valdez asks, "How bad do these chicks stink when you bust them?"

"Eh, these Asian ones in here are gonna smell alright. They get to take showers and use perfume and shit. They're gonna smell like rubbing alcohol more than anything else."

Valdez glances at him, his eyebrows raised. "No shit?"

"Yeah, it's the streetwalkers that stink," Gabriel says. "They smell like ball sweat and ass."

Valdez makes a face and lets out a low whistle. "I bet."

Laughing to himself, Gabriel starts singing with a military-style cadence, "Up in the morning with the hot Texas sunnnn, gonna FUCK all dayyyy, till the fuckin's done."

Gabriel grins at Valdez, and the two men bust up laughing, until Valdez notices a small United States Post Office truck pull up and park in the brothel's empty parking lot.

"Ohh, what do we have here?" Valdez reaches over and taps Gabriel, who is still laughing, on the shoulder with the back of his hand. "Postman making a little delivery?" The men sit up straighter, peering through the windshield, and watch as the postman exits his vehicle and walks to the side entrance.

As the postman leaves their field of view, Gabriel gets on his handheld radio. "Hey, Ter, do you see this guy?"

Teresa and Bennett are posted at the other end of the block, sitting in the front seat of a small utility van marked with a big electric company logo on the side. Four DEA agents in full tactical gear sit in the back, hidden from view. From the driver's seat, Teresa radios her response: "Yeah, we see the Postie...Tally Hoe." She un-keys and then quickly re-keys the radio. "Get it? Tally-HOE?" Barely holding back a fit of giggles, she says, "Giggity."

Her remarks get a light chuckle from the men, then Gabriel says, "Well? What is he doing?"

Teresa rolls her eyes, though Gabriel can't see her. "You're no fun."

"Teresa."

"Yeah, yeah. He rang the bell and now he's just standing there with his dick in his hand...ohh, wait...Mama San just opened up...he's in."

Valdez nods for Gabriel to give him the radio. "OK, people, we're gonna wait about ten minutes. At that point, our man here should be balls deep in KIM CHEE. Standby."

As Valdez sets the radio on the dash, Gabriel shakes his head, a scowl making the crows' feet around his eyes more pronounced.

"What?" asks Valdez.

"I don't know, bro. It's just...the guy works for the government. It'll kinda reflect badly, man."

Valdez scoffs. "Well, I didn't tell him to go get a rub and tug while he's on the fucking clock."

Just then, the radio crackles to life with Teresa's voice. "Hey Gabe, uh, you guys seeing this?"

Gabriel and Valdez look over toward the house and see a silver, luxury sedan parking next to the postal vehicle. A white man in his late thirties, wearing a polo shirt and khakis, exits the car. As the man walks toward the side entrance, Gabe radios for Teresa to advise when the man is in the house. After a few moments, Teresa informs them that a different woman let the man in.

Valdez tilts his head side to side, weighing his options, and finally sighs. "OK, how about this: Afterwards, we'll cut the postman loose and just bust Edward Jones here, huh? I just care about the drugs, I don't really give a fuck what you ICE guys do with the sex shit."

Gabriel thinks for a moment. "Yeah...yeah, we'll just say the guy was delivering the mail or something."

"OK, time on target...eight minutes," Valdez says through the radio.

Teresa acknowledges him, then looks to the men in the back. "Alright, boys, get ready."

In the passenger seat, beads of sweat roll down Bennett's temple and his leg bounces incessantly.

Upon noticing this, Teresa snorts and then pouts, pushing her bottom lip out and wrinkling up her eyebrows. "Aww, sweetie, don't be nervous. This shit isn't dangerous. There's three Asian women in there; they probably only weigh two hundred pounds put together. One dude was on his way to a fuckin' squash game, and the other doesn't want to lose his pension. The biggest danger in there is touching a used condom."

The men in the back all laugh. Bennett releases a hesitant chuckle, and some of the tension leaves his shoulders.

"Don't worry, the four TAC guys will probably catch the bullets for us, anyway," Teresa says, as she looks over her shoulder and winks at one of the DEA agents. A few minutes pass, and the agents become so silent that all one can hear is the sound of the 97-degree heat burning the outside of the van.

As Teresa and Bennett stare at the house, Valdez's voice fires up over the static of the radio: "GO!"

Inside the house, in a small, dimly lit room, the postman is naked, engaging an Asian woman atop a massage table. A small machine emits the calming sounds of ocean surf pounding against the shore, but it does little to drown out the large man's grunts as he pummels her very small frame, missionary style. He is sweating profusely, and it drips onto the woman's face. She takes it without a word, eyes shut as she forces her mind to drift elsewhere.

A loud crash resounds from somewhere else in the house. The postman freezes, listening, adrenaline flooding his system in an instant—possibly the side door of the house slamming against the wall?

A man's voice breaks the silence that followed the crash: "CLEAR!"

The small woman underneath the postman shouts at him in Chinese to get off of her, but he is now paralyzed with fear. She struggles, her own fear betrayed by her wide eyes and frantic movements, but she manages to slide out from underneath him, toward the head of the table. She overshoots and falls on her head; she cries out, but the postman only stares at the single entrance to the room, a thin wooden door.

Another crash, this time much closer. The door of the adjacent room has been kicked in. Loud voices shout, "GET ON YOUR KNEES, NOW!" and "HANDS, SHOW ME YOUR HANDS!"

Just as the prostitute manages to get to her feet, the thin door bursts open, partly knocked out of its frame. It wedges itself between the door frame and a large dresser along the same wall. As the agent in tactical gear negotiates the door obstacle, the postman can't think clearly enough to do anything other than bury his face into the padded massage table.

"Ahh, fuck," the agent mutters, then: "DON'T MOVE! SHOW ME YOUR HANDS!"

The Asian woman scrambles to put on a white coat, similar to that a doctor wears. This is common practice, to maintain the guise of providing legitimate therapeutic massages.

The agent finally shoves the door out of his way. Immediately upon entering, he puts hands on the woman. Another agent follows quickly behind and throws the postman on the ground. The agents restrain both parties with flex cuffs.

"ALL CLEAR!" is heard over the speakers of several of the tactical radios in the now seized house; at last, Agent Valdez walks in and surveys the area. From the rear door of the house enters an agent with a German Shepard. As the man and dog begin their search of the house, Gabriel enters the room housing the postman.

The postman's prostitute has been moved to another side of the house and corralled with the two other women. The postman sits on an uncomfortably small chair with his hands restrained behind his back. At least the agent who cuffed him had the decency to throw a towel over his lap. His used but empty condom lays on the floor between his legs, having slipped off with the terrified limpness that his dick now endures.

"Bad day to get some strange," Gabriel says to the postman, as though the situation is nothing more than a minor inconvenience.

The postman looks up at Gabriel, clearly scared shitless, and nods slowly.

"Sit tight, man. We'll get to you in a minute."

Gabriel joins Teresa in the other room, where the second john is. The man is almost in tears and keeps repeating, "I'm so sorry."

Teresa's head whips in the man's direction, her lips twisted in disgust. "Shut the fuck up."

Ignoring her, he begins blubbering in earnest, begging her to not arrest him.

Gabriel kicks a towel on the ground in the man's direction. "She said, *shut up*." Turning to Teresa, he asks, "Where's Bennett?"

"He's with the whores." She nods toward the other end of the hall.

The second john pleads to Gabriel, sensing that he is in charge. "Please don't arrest me. I didn't do anything!"

Gabriel scoffs, incredulous. "Do you always wear a condom when you get a massage? This fucking guy," he says to Teresa, shaking his head. To the john, he says, "Her DNA is on a condom that was found on your cock, man. There is no getting out of this. We got our interpreter in there with her now. That girl is seventeen, bro! You're going away."

That does it for the man, and he breaks down. Teresa and Gabriel leave the room to get away from the pathetic scene. They nod to the agent in TAC gear who remains to stand guard as they pass.

"Interpreter? I'm not convinced the new guy fully speaks English," Teresa jokes as they walk, earning a grin from Gabriel. They join up with Valdez in a makeshift apartment the three women were using it as their living quarters when not with a client, found deeper within the house. It is now being torn apart by a crime scene technician searching for the desired contraband.

"Found anything yet?" asks Gabriel.

With an increasingly frustrated tone, Valdez replies, "Not yet, but the dog isn't done." He rubs a hand gruffly down his face. "Ahh, maybe we got bad intel."

"Don't worry, bro. If shit's here, the dog will find it."

As the three make their way back toward the front of the house, the agent with the dog informs Valdez that there is no sign of drugs in the house. "Search it again. Start over. Check their fucking snatches if you have to, but find the drugs!" Valdez shouts as he points at the row of stoic prostitutes sitting along the kitchen wall.

For a second, it seems as if the agent with the dog will backtalk Valdez, but instead he clenches his jaw and begins his search again.

"What about our boy?" Gabriel asks Valdez.

"Yeah, sure, cut him loose. Let Wall Street douche take the pop," Valdez replies, all the steam gone from him.

"Good man," says Gabriel, and he smacks Valdez on the side of his arm.

Teresa and Gabriel return to the room with the postman and relieve his guard. As the agent in TAC gear exits the room, Gabriel's face grows serious and he holds the postman's eyes with a stern glare. "You were just delivering the mail. Got it?"

The shocked postman stares at Gabriel in a suspended moment of disbelief, then nods his head. Gabriel gestures to Teresa, and she swiftly flips open her pocket knife.

"Lean forward, big guy," she says as she grips his flex cuffs and begins to cut him loose. After the postman is freed from his binds, he hastily grabs his clothes and begins to dress. Once he is in full uniform, albeit disheveled, the three exit the room and walk toward the side entrance to the house.

Outside, the agent with the dog is searching the exterior of the house. A perimeter of yellow police tape has been erected and a few onlookers have gathered. Trying to help the postman save face, Gabriel extends his hand to shake the postman's, and says loud enough for the onlookers to hear, "Thanks for the help!"

The postman, still not sure what's happening, shakes Gabriel's hand and says, "Thank you."

As the postman walks toward his truck, Valdez emerges from the house, his frustration finally overflowing as he begins to berate the agent with the dog. "Did you feed it? Maybe it needs to take a shit!"

The scolded agent opens his mouth to retort, heading for Valdez to address his insulting tone, when the dog suddenly strains against his leash, pulling the agent toward the driveway.

The postman is almost to his truck when Valdez sees what's got the dog all hot under the collar. "Freeze!" Valdez takes off at a run toward the postman, who is stupid enough to attempt fleeing when he realizes they're on to him. "I said, FREEZE, FUCKER!"

His attempt is short-lived; Valdez tackles him to the ground, the two men rolling to a stop on the pavement. Freedom was so close for the postman, and he knows it. After a search of the truck yields four keys of cocaine, handcuffs are once again put on his wrists.

Once the postal truck is fully processed and Valdez feels that the DEA's work is done, he orders his men to pack up and head back to their office. The crime scene is now in the hands of Gabriel and his team. Bennett and Teresa have already left to transport the females to the processing facility, and Gabriel will take the second john to lockup.

Gabriel closes the back door of his car after securing the second john, then walks over toward Valdez, who's sitting in his SUV. "Look, bro, I'm sorry. I almost fucked us bad there."

"No worries. How could you have known? All that matters to my bosses is that I got some drugs on the table," replies Valdez as he starts the ignition.

"Alright, bro." Gabriel attempts to slap hands goodbye with Valdez, and the DEA agent returns the favor.

As he walks away, Valdez calls to him: "Hey, Gabe...one more thing, man." Gabriel stops, turning back toward the vehicle.

"It's a good thing that you only go to the Mexican shops, huh? You could have gotten pretty jammed up if you had fucked here before." Valdez shoots him a smile and then drives off before Gabriel can reply. He's left alone, stunned, as he watches the truck disappear down the road.

CHAPTER FIVE

R O S A L I E ' S C R O S S I N G

Located fifty miles southwest of the Laredo, Texas border crossing sits the town of Anáhuac. With a population of 17,000, this town is a prime staging point for most cartel incursions into the United States.

An old Toyota Tercel pulls up to the curb outside a dilapidated warehouse. The building is riddled with bullet holes and parts of the roof are missing, the small parking lot strewn with debris and tumbleweeds. As Rosalie sits in the back seat with another young woman, she attempts to look through her window toward the burnt-out building, but she is blinded by the reflection of bright sunlight from a shard of broken glass in a blown-out window high up on the wall. She can only make out the silhouette of a man standing in a doorway.

As their courier exits the driver's side, she hears a muffled conversation taking place between the courier and the man from the doorway. As the man approaches the car, she can now see that he is white. Older, quite possibly in his fifties, he has a thick head of snow-white hair and a large gut. As she looks the man up and down, he greets the courier. The men appear to know each other and converse in a jovial manner. After a few moments of conversation, the white man claps his hands loudly and smiles, coming closer to the car.

The courier gets to Rosalie's door first and opens it. The courier orders the two young women out of the car. As she exits the vehicle, she is once again blinded by the unrelenting sunlight. When her eyes begin to adjust, she looks up at the white man's face. Rosalie's breath hitches: He is staring at her, a sinister smile on his face. With her heart now racing, she forces herself to be still when his fingers lightly brush under her chin.

Speaking in Spanish, the white man's voice is clear and strong without the barrier of the car door between them: "Ahh, you've brought me a real treasure, my friend."

Looking at Rosalie, the courier's eyebrows knit together, and he says, "I don't know about that one. She's been coughing the whole fucking trip."

Upon hearing this, Rosalie forces a few fake coughs to keep up her charade.

Unfazed, the white man says, "A little cough never hurt anybody. Besides, she'll get plenty of fresh air out in the fields."

The men share a laugh that makes Rosalie's blood run cold. Still, she does not let her demeanor betray her fear.

To the girls, the courier introduces the white man as "Cucuy." The irony of the white man choosing to call himself the "Boogeyman" is that it doesn't scare Rosalie. As a young girl, she would have nightmares about monsters coming to take her in the night. Her mother and father showed her that it was just the sound of an ash tree brushing against the side of their house causing these fears. After that, the nightmares ended.

Momentarily, she drifts off in that memory, overcome with a visceral reaction to the thought of her mother's touch and her father's gentle smile as they comforted her. She is snapped back to reality with a harsh, bitter clarity as the courier informs her and the other girl that they will belong to the white man for the next part of their journey. The lie that the young women will simply be migrant workers is still played out. The girls acquiesce, and the courier closes the back door of the car.

"You need anything else?" asks the courier.

"No, I think we will be fine. Thank you." Cucuy grins at the girls as he speaks, never taking his eyes off Rosalie. As the courier drives away, leaving a small whirlwind of dust in the air, Cucuy sandwiches himself between the two young girls, curling an arm around each and hugging them tightly to his sides. As he walks them toward the building, he reassures them that everything will be better when they get to the United States.

Once inside the building, Rosalie can see several old mattresses scattered across the floor. Support poles are the only decorative features in the otherwise desolate place. The air is so acrid that it is almost visible to the naked eye. A small, handheld radio hangs by a carrying strap from a nail in the wall. An American station plays faintly through the static.

Giving the girls a slight squeeze, his face tilted toward Rosalie so that his breath blows moist in her ear, Cucuy kindly asks, "What are your names?"

"Celeste," says the other girl.

Rosalie remains silent as she looks up at a hole in the ceiling.

"And what about you, my love?" As Cucuy speaks, he gently begins to run his hand down Rosalie's back, stopping when he gets to the top of her butt.

Trying to avoid her body's urge to tense up and under the gross tickle of his breath and recoil from his hand, she hesitates before saying, "Rosalie, señor," with a slight cough.

Cucuy laughs at the cough as he looks at her, openly skeptical of her "illness." For a moment, she is afraid he will say something about it. However, he releases them from his grasp and turns to Celeste.

He says, "What we are going to do now is, I'm going to take Rosalie here across the border into the United States. I can only take one girl at a time, so I will have to leave you here, Celeste." As he speaks, he removes a pair of handcuffs from a bag near one of the support poles, and gently grabs Celeste's right hand. He walks the girl to one of the support poles, and as he handcuffs her hands together around it, Rosalie can see the girl is trembling from head to toe. Cucuy motions for Celeste to sit down on the mattress next her. As she slowly and awkwardly squats down onto the mattress, a tribe of cockroaches scatters.

Cucuy turns and walks a few feet away, to a small plastic bucket. He grabs it and brings it to Celeste. Inside the bucket are four bottles of water and two cans of garbanzo beans with pop-tops. "This is for you to use when you need to pee and...well...you know. I suggest you take out the water and beans before you do that, though." He lets out a guttural laugh, his gut bouncing. Serious again, he tells Celeste, "You will be here until this same time tomorrow. I can only cross one time per day."

The girl's bottom lip begins to quiver, confusion and terror in her eyes as they flick from Cucuy to Rosalie and back again. Rosalie's stoicism breaks for just a second as she stares at Celeste, chained up like an animal, and she fights the urge to cry. Refusing to let tears fall, she takes her eyes from Celeste and watches Cucuy instead, willing herself to muster the resolve to survive whatever awaits her.

He walks to the radio and removes it from the nail. As he walks back toward Celeste, he adjusts the tuning knob so that the station comes through more clearly. "You ladies like 80s music?" he asks.

Rosalie opens and closes her mouth, shocked at the absurdity of the question. As she watches him, she wants to run, but finds her feet rooted to the ground; even through the panic setting in, she knows that will bring nothing but pain.

"One love feeds the fire. One heart burns desire..." emits from the speaker as Cucuy turns up the volume, then tosses the radio onto the mattress with Celeste.

When he turns back to Rosalie, there's a wolfish gleam in his eye. She feels light-headed as he approaches her, and she takes a small, involuntary step back. He puts a hand on each of her shoulders and gives them a light squeeze; her retreat seems to egg him on, and a smile turns up the corners of his mouth. "It will be a few hours in the car, and I will need you to be absolutely quiet. No one can even hear you breathe. Do you understand?"

She simply and emphatically nods, unable to speak. She is starting to understand what will come next.

He smiles at her, and his hand comes up to brush the side of her neck, then cradles her cheek against its palm. Simultaneously, his left hand finds her hip and he pulls her closer, squishing her against his gut.

Her heart pounding now, she remembers her mother's advice and begins to hack furiously. She tries to sound convincing, which isn't difficult because she can hardly breathe in the first place.

Cucuy is undeterred. "Stop that, beautiful." His left hand slides longingly up her side, then around and down to her lower back. "I've got the poison in me and I need to get it out." His eyelids grow heavy as his gaze lands on her chest; he is mesmerized by the rapid rising and falling of her breasts. Without warning, he dips his head to her neck, savagely kissing the tender skin there. The assault causes her shoulders to tense up, rising nearly to her ears, and the hand against her cheek slithers into her hair, grabbing a fistful of it and yanking her head to the side to allow him access to her neck again.

He moans against her skin as he picks her up and lays her down on the closest mattress. Rosalie scans the room frantically, hoping for anything that might help her, but all she finds is Celeste, wide-eyed as she watches, tears streaming down her face. Cucuy straddles Rosalie, already unbuttoning his shirt. Unable to hold it off any longer, the first sob tears itself from her chest as she tries to free herself by pushing at his groin, attempting to roll him off of her with her hips. Her fists beat wildly against his chest.

He stops unbuttoning his shirt to grab her wrists, pinning them to the mattress on either side of her head. She struggles against him hopelessly as he leans down to her ear. "You little bitch," he spits venomously, all charade of the nice older man left behind. "Do you want us to kill your family? Keep it up, and you will end up at the bottom of a hole."

She freezes, staring once again at the hole in the ceiling. Images of her father, face-down in the dirt, flash through her mind and the fight leaves her body in a sudden flush.

Satisfied that he's made his point, Cucuy's demeanor abruptly switches back, and he smiles as he finishes removing his shirt. He stands up to remove his khaki shorts. Now completely nude, and convinced she will not try to escape again, he stands over Rosalie. She imagines she can feel his eyes like a laser burning her flesh as they travel over her body—and then he is back on the mattress, unbuttoning her pants, and in a move that was surely practiced on many young girls before her, he strips her from the waist down in one swift motion, leaving her lower half completely exposed. He throws the wad of clothing across the room. In his haste to begin, he allows her to keep her shirt on.

Without any semblance of care, the man thrusts himself into the delicate young girl, effectively deflowering her and inducing a bloodcurdling scream that rips through the building, echoing off the walls. Her heels dig into the mattress, trying desperately to push her body out from under Cucuy. As her back arches against the blistering agony below her waist and her legs begin to shake, unable to take the pain, her head rolls to the side and she sees Celeste. The other girl is huddled on her mattress, her legs drawn up and her face buried in her knees. Cucuy begins to move faster and Rosalie's skin tears with the friction. Another scream bursts from Rosalie, and Celeste's shoulders begin to shake violently as she cries; with her arms extended painfully before her, she has no reprieve from Rosalie's wails.

The tormented girl's screams become muffled as Cucuy puts his large hand over the lower half of Rosalie's face, nearly smothering her. In the throes of terror, his threats forgotten, she punches the sides of his head as she struggles to breathe. She gains relief for the briefest of moments when he releases her face, and she draws in a lungful of air, only to be struck hard across her cheek by the same hand. In shock, Rosalie goes very still and finds the hole in the ceiling, tears still sliding into her hair.

To the music of the radio, Rosalie silently endures the final short, stabbing thrusts of the pale, fat man. Minutes later, he stands over her again, this time yanking his shorts back up, a satisfied smirk on his face. He looks at her almost lovingly for a moment, and Rosalie closes her eyes and curls into a ball, her whole body shivering convulsively.

Heaving a big sigh, Cucuy wipes the sweat off of his forehead and walks over to the jumble of Rosalie's pants and underwear. As he begins to button his shirt, he kicks the ball of clothes at Rosalie. It hits her in her back.

"Get dressed! We have to get going," he barks in Spanish. He walks over to Celeste's bucket and takes a bottle of water, opening it and chugging it feverishly.

Still lying on her side, curled into herself, Rosalie untangles her clothes. With trembling hands, she pulls her underwear up, then stands to put on her pants. Her legs are shaking so furiously still, she nearly falls several times before she is able to get the pants all the way up and secure the button.

Cucuy finishes the water and throws the bottle on the ground. "Hurry up. Let's go," he commands again. He heads for the door.

In fear of reprimand, Rosalie scrambles to follow, wincing at the foreign, painful way her body now moves. Before she exits the building, she looks back at Celeste. The girl is still weeping softly, and won't look at Rosalie. She feels compelled to apologize to Celeste, and utters, "I'm sorry."

Outside, Cucuy leads Rosalie to a large SUV that appears to be brand new. He opens the passenger side door and points to where the dashboard should be. The dashboard has been removed, and many of the interior components have been gutted. The console has been hollowed out to form a small alcove, large enough for a small woman to fit in—with barely enough room for her to breathe. Cucuy orders her to lay down in the recess.

Rosalie is still devastated from the trauma that she just endured; her legs feel like rubber, her mind as though she is drunk. She doesn't move.

"Get up there!" says Cucuy again as he points at the dash.

She flinches at his tone, afraid he might hit her again, and steps forward, but she is unsure how she is supposed to enter the small, awkward space.

Cucuy huffs his irritation with her and shoves her forward. "Just lay on your right side with your head toward the steering wheel."

She attempts to do as he says, however, once she is laying on her side in the recess, her legs stick out in a cumbersome way. "Bend your knees, damn it!" Cucuy shouts as he forces her knees to bend so that her heels are pressed against her butt. Rosalie holds the painful pose, and just like the last piece of a puzzle, she fits snugly inside.

Cucuy grabs the thinned-out dashboard top from the back of the SUV. As he is about to place the panel overtop Rosalie, essentially entombing her for the duration of the ride, he reiterates for her to be quiet no matter what. She is to not make a sound until he lets her out on the other side. Rosalie closes her eyes instead of answering, going someplace deep within her mind as she resigns herself to the trip.

Her silence is acknowledgment enough for Cucuy. He lays the panel down in its place and begins to screw in a series of tactfully placed screws throughout the dash. After the last screw is in, he walks back to the building and throws the screwdriver inside. "I'll be back tomorrow," he says to Celeste, then he closes the building door and padlocks it shut.

46

He gets in the SUV and drives to the main road, en route to the border. An hour's drive later, they arrive. The line at the checkpoint is especially long today. Cucuy begins to complain to himself about the lack of air conditioning, due to the vehicle's gutted components, as he digs around in the center console for a collection of random items to scatter across the dashboard. An old baseball hat and a crinkled-up paper bag from a fast food restaurant complete the dashboard's camouflage. After what feels like an eternity to him, he pulls up to a U.S. Immigration officer. As Cucuy hands the officer his driver's license and passport card, he greets the officer with a warm smile. "Officer Derringer, how are you doing today, man?"

The officer responds in kind. "Jeff, how are you? How are those treatments coming?" The officer glances over Cucuy's documents, which show he is actually Jeffrey Floding, of Laredo, Texas, before handing them back. He's seen them many times before.

"Ahh, I'd complain, but who'd listen? The doctors in Laredo said I had a year to live, at best, but these Mexican doctors say"— Cucuy pauses to look at an official-looking medical document from a manila folder on the passenger seat—"my Cancer is in aggressive remission."

Officer Derringer laughs and shakes his head. "Doctors don't know shit. They said my grandma had two months to live—the bitch lived for another four years. Breaking her hip in the shower is what finally did her in."

As Cucuy and the officer talk, another immigration officer walks around the vehicle with a mirror at the end of a pole, checking

R. A. McCAIN

the underside of the SUV. Officer Derringer casually looks into the backseat area as he hands the two forms of ID back to Cucuy. "How often does that doc have you coming down for treatment now?"

"Seems like whenever he needs money," Cucuy says, chuckling at his own wit. "About three times a week. I'll be back down tomorrow, but after that I can't come for almost two weeks because of work."

Remembering that the line is backed up to eternity, and feeling a piercing glare from his supervisor, Officer Derringer nods and says, "Alright, well, feel better, man."

With typical departing pleasantries and a smile, Cucuy drives on. His cover story of a man going to Mexico for cheap cancer treatment has succeeded once again, as it has so many times in the past, and his fragile contraband remains safe and sound in the hidden compartment.

Rosalie Bolanos has entered the land of the free, and is once again afraid of the Boogeyman.

CHAPTER SIX
THE VIGILANTE

Troy Menard is a thirty-two-year-old man with a wife and an eight-year-old daughter. Growing up a white man in the affluent community of River Oaks sheltered him from much of the awfulness of the world. Now, with a newfound sense of duty, he feels it's his burden to do what the police have so obviously failed to do. He has become "The River Oaks Vigilante."

It's 9 p.m. on a Sunday night. Troy feels an even greater sense of contempt for the whore mongers today than he does on other day of the week; today is the Lord's day, and it's being sullied by the sodomites across the street. It's not only his religious convictions that drive Troy forward in his quest, though. Every time he looks at his daughter's face, he can't help but think about the poor women that have been stolen from their families and sold into slavery.

With his camera at the ready, he patiently sits in the driver's seat of his hatchback. Parked in the driveway of an abandoned house, he has the windows down on this surprisingly temperate evening. He glances up from his phone from time to time to check the parking lot of the brothel across the street. The lot is empty, though a neon sign in the brothel's front window flashes "OPEN," and he wonders for a moment if his campaign is starting to bear fruit; not a single customer has been by since he began his stakeout two hours ago. He looks back down to his phone and continues playing a game.

Focusing intently on the game, he fails to notice that two men have approached his car. Both men are Hispanic, dressed in stylish business suits. One of the men walks around to the passenger side and quickly reaches through the window, grabbing Troy's camera. With a delayed reaction, Troy is too late in trying to stop the man from taking it.

Instead, he attempts to start the vehicle and flee, but he is too late again: The hard jab of what feels like the barrel of a handgun is digging into his left side.

In a harsh, low tone, the man with the gun tells Troy to stop and remove the key from the ignition. Troy complies, and a nervous tremor in his hand causes him to drop the keys as he does so.

The man holding Troy's camera opens the passenger side door and sits down in the car. As he closes the door, he casually says, "Ohh, man. It's a nice night tonight. Not a cloud in the sky."

The first tendrils of real fear take hold in Troy, but he keeps his bearings. Remaining straight faced, he nods in acknowledgement of the man's words.

"Ahh, look at me, being rude. I'm Gustavo." The man in the passenger seat extends his right hand to shake Troy's.

Troy keeps his hands where they are, firmly gripping the steering wheel, his contempt for Gustavo showing in the set of his jaw.

"That's alright. We don't need to be friends." Gustavo retracts his hand and goes back to inspecting the camera. He holds it up, gesturing toward Troy with it as he says, "We came out here tonight to tell you how much we admire your photography. You take some really good pictures, man."

Gustavo looks through the aperture and points the lens toward the brothel. "Ahh, me, I'm no good at taking pictures. I'm more of a video guy." Suddenly changing gears, he lays the camera on his lap and removes a large smartphone from his blazer's interior pocket and holds it out to Troy. "I don't know if it's any good, but why don't you check out my most recent work?"

Troy accepts the phone with an unsteady hand, a sick feeling taking root in his gut. As Gustavo lifts the camera up again and looks through the aperture, this time rotating the barrel of the lens as if he is really going to take a picture, Troy looks at the screen of the smart phone.

His hand flies up to his mouth and he draws a quick, sharp breath through his nose—it's a still image of his wife. She is on her knees, bound and gagged. Just from the still, it is clear that there is blood streaming down her face from her left eye, which is bruised and swollen.

He presses the play button.

In the video, his wife's chest rises and falls rapidly with heavy, shallow breaths and her good eye is wide with terror. He can hear his daughter weeping out of frame from somewhere nearby. As the camera pans right, his daughter's whimpering becomes more audible. Troy recognizes the background—it's the kitchen in his house. His breathing intensifies as tears begin to pool in his eyes.

Gustavo lowers the camera and looks over toward the screen. "That's a nice house, man. I really like the backsplash you guys put in."

Troy jerks his head to stare at Gustavo for a moment, shocked to hear such ordinary chitchat. The moment passes and he returns to the video; his daughter is now in frame. She is also gagged, her hands tied behind her back. She sits on the floor with her legs crossed and is not visibly injured.

The camera pans back to Troy's wife. The cameraman's hand can be seen reaching toward her, and it jerks the gag out of her mouth.

"Tell your husband to stop," says a menacing voice off camera.

"Troy, please stop. Please, come home," she whimpers. A sob racks Troy's body, but he quickly regains his composure, freezing as he sees the cameraman's hand once again—this time the hand is brandishing a knife. At first, his wife becomes very still, a look of resignation on her face, then her whole body jolts, and with wild eyes she shouts, "PLEASE, NO!" as the knife and the camera move toward their daughter. As the knife approaches his daughters face, the video suddenly stops, and the screen goes black.

When Gustavo speaks, his tone has changed from that of a casual and playful man to a more serious one. "Are you done fucking with us now?"

"Yes, yes! Please, don't hurt my family!" Tears spill down Troy's face as he pleads frantically, "Tell me my girl is OK."

Gustavo chuckles at Troy's reaction. "They are fine. Your wife might want to ice down her eye, but they are fine." He takes the phone back from Troy, then flips through it and calls a number.

As someone on the other end answers, Gustavo says, "We're good," and waits for a reply. A moment later, he hangs up the phone. "They left your wife and daughter tied up in a closet."

Troy lets out a sigh of relief, but Gustavo isn't finished.

"If you get the idea to go to the police or the FBI, or what have you, I'd think twice. Your wife is too fucking ugly for us to turn out, so we'll probably just cut her head off, but that daughter of yours is a cutie pie. You don't want her to become a whore...do you?" Gustavo asks, his tone casual as if he is merely inquiring what Troy would like for dinner.

Rapidly shaking his head, Troy's voice quivers as he begs, "No, please—NO!"

Gustavo's partner leans down, his head slightly through the driver's side window, and aks, "Why aren't we just gonna kill this fucking idiot?"

Troy's breath hitches as he waits for Gustavo's reply.

Gustavo glares at Troy. "No, *mano*, too much blood in the water attracts pigs. This little bitch won't be a problem now."

As Gustavo opens his door and exits the vehicle, he holds up Troy's camera, then forcefully throws it on the ground, breaking it into several pieces.

The men walk off, disappearing into the night as Troy feverishly searches for his keys. Breathing heavily now, Troy finds the keys in the footwell and starts the car. He speeds away, heading back to his house across town. As he recklessly drives along the highway, he tries to call his wife's cell phone. There is no answer, but he keeps trying anyway.

His wheels screech as he pulls haphazardly into his driveway. The house is pitch-black, not even the porch light on. He attempts to unlock the front door, but with shaky hands it takes him several tries. When he finally unlocks the door, he runs inside, calling out for his wife and daughter as he frantically checks every closet and every room on his way through the house. He continues upstairs, adrenaline mixing with the fear that Gustavo lied; he still hasn't heard a sound. Eventually, the master bedroom is the only possible place left, and he braces himself for what he might find as he shoves the door open.

He turns on the bedroom light, quickly scans the empty room, and runs to the closet door. Opening it, he finds instant relief: His wife and daughter are still alive. Huddled together in the large walk-in closet, they are both still bound and gagged. As she looks up at him, his wife's body relaxes and she whimpers.

"Oh my god, I'm so happy to see you guys." He shushes his daughter, who has begun crying again, though she's smiling behind her gag. "I'm here now. I'm here. Hold on."

As Troy kneels down to free them, his wife and daughter's demeanor changes again. As he looks at them, confused, the last thing Troy sees, before his brains are splattered across his family, is his wife screaming though her gag. His body falls forward lifelessly, landing across his wife and child.

Two more muffled gunshots burst from the muzzle and his wife and daughter are sent to meet him in the afterlife. Outside, Gustavo and his partner wait in a running car. The shooter exits the house and gets in the back seat. The three men drive away, and so ends the crusade of the River Oaks Vigilante.

CHAPTER SEVEN
THE SHOWER

A black sedan pulls up and parks in front of an "American Foursquare"-style house. A man in his thirties exits the driver's side. The man is Hispanic and slender, dressed all in black. He closes the car door and walks around to the other side. As the man walks around the front of the car, he adjusts his skin-tight shirt by tucking the back into his pants. He surveys the area as he opens the passenger side door, then he bends over and removes two large bags of Chinese take-out. He closes the door and walks toward the house. As he approaches the front door, it opens for him, and he walks in uninterrupted.

A middle-aged Hispanic woman greets him happily: "Luis, thank God. I'm so hungry."

Luis smiles at the woman as they pass through the dingy, sparsely decorated living room and continue down the hall toward the kitchen.

Alger is sitting at the kitchen table, thumbing through an old magazine. As Luis sets the bags of food on the table, Alger looks up and grins. "Ahh, you are a life saver, *mano*. For a minute there, I thought I'd have to eat Elena's cooking."

The woman, Elena, glares at Alger as she retrieves some plastic cups and paper plates from the cupboard.

Rodrigo enters the room, wearing a white undershirt and red athletic shorts. "Mmm, Chinese. *Gracias, mano.*"

As the men sit around the table and begin to distribute the food, Elena fills their cups with soda. "Did you wash the girls yet?" asks Luis to the group.

"Nahh, not yet. We know how you like to watch," Alger says before he bites into an egg roll.

Luis looks to Rodrigo. "Why don't you go get them, so Elena can get them started?"

Annoyed at the order, Rodrigo still attempts a respectful tone. "Can't I eat first?"

"I have an appointment across town and don't have a lot of time." Luis stares at Rodrigo, daring the subordinate man to challenge him again.

Alger and Elena watch Rodrigo, motionless, shocked that he would question an order. Several moments pass as Luis and Rodrigo stare each other down, but at last Rodrigo caves and puts down his uneaten egg roll and walks to the back door.

Outside, out of view from his superior, Rodrigo doesn't bother to hide his anger. His steps are heavy and he mutters curses under his breath as he makes his way through the back yard, which is surrounded by a tall privacy fence to ward off prying eyes, to a small shed in the back corner. He enters the combination on the padlock and removes it, then slams the metal flap over. As he opens the door, sunlight illuminates the women spread out in the small space. Each woman's back is pressed up against a wall, trying to get as far away from the nearly full bucket of human waste in the center of the shed as possible.

"*Vamos*," Rodrigo barks in a low tone.

The women are quick to rise; most are happy because they know it's time for a shower and a meal. The women file into the house and Rodrigo closes the door behind them.

Elena stands when the first girl enters the kitchen, and she leads the line of women upstairs.

As they file past Luis, he stares at them like a child watching a parade. An altogether different expression, something closer to shock, takes over his face when he sees Rosalie walk by. He grabs a pint of the Chinese food and slowly follows the last girl in the line upstairs.

Without wasting any time, Elena tells the women to remove all of their clothes and put them in a large trash bag that she hands to one of them. Luis watches from the doorway of the empty bedroom, leaning against the frame and casually eating from the container in his hand, as they begin stripping off their dingy sundresses and muumuus. Now naked, the eight women stand listlessly as they wait while Elena takes the bag of soiled clothes and ties it up.

Elena guides the first girl into a nearby bathroom. As Elena can be heard telling the woman how to shower properly, Luis stares half in wonder, half in lust at the naked Rosalie.

Rosalie stands beneath the air conditioning vent, shivering against the rush of cool air. Even after all she has endured, she is still bashful and attempts to cover her exposed breasts with her arms.

From down the hall, Elena calls for the next girl. Rosalie jumps at the opportunity and walks toward the door. She can feel Luis' eyes gazing at her, and she avoids making eye contact, praying she will make it by him without interaction.

As she nears Luis and the doorway, he sticks his arm out and forms a barrier. Rosalie stops, but remains looking straight ahead.

"What is your name?"

Her voice is little more than a whisper. "Rosalie."

He grabs her forearm and pulls it away to expose her breasts, but keeps it in his grasp. Rosalie forces herself to stay calm as he looks her up and down. From the periphery of her vision, she watches him; he doesn't appear to be looking at her for sexual satisfaction. Instead, he's looking at her much the same way a rancher would scan for quality livestock. He releases her hand and grabs her face, forcing her to look at him. After a few moments of looking into her eyes, he releases her and nods for her to go shower. Rosalie exhales a pent-up breath and walks swiftly to the bathroom.

Luis grimaces as he looks at his hands and rubs his fingers together; they are now dirty.

Rodrigo and Alger are still gorging themselves on the half-eaten food when Luis returns to the kitchen. As he walks to the sink and begins to wash his hands, he asks, "That new girl. Is she the one that the white man brought the other day?"

Alger answers through a mouthful of food, his lips smacking obnoxiously as he says, "Yes, he brought her by two nights ago."

Now drying his hands with a dishtowel, Luis turns around to face the two men. A moment of silence passes as they continue to chew their food, paying him little attention, and then: "Did you two idiots ever think that she is too beautiful to be selling for ten dollars a fuck?"

Alger winces at the sharpness of Luis' voice, and his superior throws the wet dishtowel at him. Both men stop eating as the towel hits Alger across the face and falls to the ground. He and Rodrigo stare submissively at Luis.

"A girl that *quality* should be in our spa," Luis shouts, growing furious. He slams his hands down on the table, making the food cartons jump and scatter, as he growls, "A girl that *quality* should be getting us two hundred dollars a fuck!"

Both Alger and Rodrigo remain silent, humbly watching their boss as they wait for his outburst to pass.

Straightening, Luis takes a deep breath and reaches into his pocket, retrieving his car keys. "OK. I'm gonna leave now. I'm gonna call Hector and tell him that you are going to bring that one by at four o'clock. You can do it on the way to the spot."

As Luis walks toward the front door to leave, Alger jumps out of his chair to walk him out. Once the door is shut and Luis is gone, Alger makes his way upstairs. As he passes through the kitchen, he sees Rodrigo hurl his metal fork against the wall. He ignores Rodrigo, feeling anger of his own taking hold.

Alger finds Elena in the bathroom, where the last girl has just finished showering. As Elena towels the girl off, Alger says, "Wash that new *puta* again!"

Elena glances at him but continues what she's doing. "Which one?"

"Rosalie, you dumb bitch. Make sure her pussy is really clean. We're moving her to the Spa," Alger barks.

Elena pauses in shock for a moment, unsure if she heard him correctly, then resumes drying off the girl standing before her. Aware she is at the low end of the totem pole, she simply says, "OK."

After Alger has gone back downstairs, Elena and the last girl return to the bedroom and Elena opens a giant rubber bin in the closet. She removes various sundresses and muumuus from the bin and begins tossing them at each of the girls. After each of the girls, save for Rosalie, has an article of clothing and has dressed, Elena retrieves two medium-sized trash cans from the closet. One is clean, with no liner, and contains dozens of cans of food. The other is empty except for a trash bag. "Take a can and eat. When you are done, throw the can in this," Elena instructs them as she points to the trash can that has a liner.

Rosalie attempts to grab a can of food, but Elena stops her. "No, little girl. You need another bath."

Elena grabs Rosalie by the wrist and yanks her back toward the door. As Rosalie is pulled from the bedroom, she watches the other girls popping the tops off the cans and happily pouring the food into their mouths, and her stomach growls painfully.

Elena practically throws Rosalie back in the tub and tells her to sit down. As the woman turns on the faucet, she mocks Rosalie. "Looks like you are special. Looks like you don't have to go to the field anymore."

Rosalie's head snaps up and she stares at Elena, wondering what that could mean. Better or worse?

Elena grabs a washrag and squirts a glob of body soap onto it. As she closes her hand around it, mashing the soap into the rag, she holds the clenched fist close to Rosalie's face. "No matter how hot this water gets, or how much soap I use, you will never be clean," Elena sneers at the girl. "You aren't special. You are just a dumb little whore."

Suddenly, Elena shoves her hand between Rosalie's legs and begins to clean her most private of parts with a rough and heavy hand. Rosalie winces, trying hard not to cry out in pain, as Elena watches her with a cruel smile. Elena revels in the satisfaction of knowing that she is no longer a whore.

The same can't be said for Rosalie; her journey to the bottom is only beginning.

CHAPTER EIGHT
THE GARDENERS

Ulrika Granado, "Oolie" to her friends and family, is thirty-six years old. She has been married to Gabriel for two years, and they have no children. Originally from Germany, Gabriel met her through an international matchmaking website. Even he finds it ironic that an Immigration agent would marry a foreign woman, whom he met only a handful of times prior—one whom most people would categorize as a mail-order bride.

Early on, their marriage was great. However, certain cultural differences and the lack of familiar faces in the United States have made Oolie grow increasingly hostile. They have been fighting for months; it was Gabriel's long work hours that finally brought tensions to a boiling point.

Although he does works long, irregular hours, he is not always working when he tells her that he is.

The sounds of lawnmowers and weed whackers provide a backdrop as Gabriel and Oolie argue in their living room. It's hot and only growing hotter, and every window in the house is open. The curtains sway with a light breeze. "Well, maybe if you didn't run the air conditioner twenty-four seven, we would have gotten more than three years out of the fucking thing!" Gabriel yells, throwing his arms up in frustration.

"I am from Germany, not fa-king Tex-ass. I can't stand this goddamn heat!" Tired and upset, Oolie crosses her arms over her chest, and he can tell she is about to check out of the argument.

He lets out a heavy sigh. "When did the A/C guy say he was gonna be here?"

"The lady said he was busy and can't be here until four o'clock."

"Jesus fucking Christ, that's two and a half hours from now! You couldn't call another repair place?" Gabriel fumes.

"I call number on home warranty paper. You want to spend more money, so be it. I'm going to swim in pool now." Oolie waves her hand dismissively as she walks out the back door onto the patio, spewing expletives under her breath in her native tongue.

Gabriel walks into the kitchen and deflates as he opens the refrigerator. He peers inside, enjoying the light rush of cool air on his face, then grabs a bottle of water and closes the door. He walks over to the kitchen sink, where he can see Oolie out of a small, open window. She has removed her t-shirt and shorts to reveal her slightly pudgy body, now covered by nothing more than a bikini. Gabriel marvels at what two short years in America have done to her once athletic physique.

As he drinks the water and watches his wife step into the pool, he hears two Mexican gardeners along the side of the house. They have finished mowing the lawn and are now raking up grass clippings, talking to one another in Spanish.

"Fucking rich white bitch. Look at her fat ass swimming in that pool," says the older of the two men.

The younger man stops momentarily and watches her swim. "I'd like to lay that pale bitch down and eat that pussy for days."

The older man rests his arm atop the handle of his rake and leans in conspiratorially. "Nahh, brother. Those white bitches are too high maintenance. I know a place where you can fuck a good piece of Mexican pussy for only ten dollars."

Already eavesdropping with minimal interest, the last comment has gotten Gabriel's complete attention.

"For real?" asks the younger man.

"Yeah, man. Let's go after work. We'll go get some *panocha* and a bottle of tequila."

The younger man seems hesitant. "I don't know…"

"OK, we'll get two bottles of tequila!" They both laugh as they move toward the front of the house, out of ear-shot.

Gabriel waits for the two men to go around front, then walks out on the back patio and tells Oolie, "I can't wait for that fucking thing to get fixed. I'm going out. The checkbook is on the counter."

Oolie glances at him over her shoulder and then turns her head away, giving him the silent treatment.

No longer interested in his wife, he ignores her attitude and makes his way to the garage. Hoping he hasn't missed them, he gets in his small pickup truck. As the garage door opens, he looks in his rearview mirror; he can see the two men packing the lawn equipment into the back of a trailer attached to a large pickup truck. As the two men and three other gardeners jump into the bed of the truck, Gabriel begins to pull out of his garage.

He follows the truck from a safe distance as they go from job to job. After three hours of watching the group mow lawns in various neighborhoods, he senses that they are done for the day. He follows the crew to the parking lot of a large home repair store. The two men he is surveilling exit the truck and are given their day's wages by the driver.

They walk to a parked piece-of-shit SUV and get inside. The engine turns over after a few attempts, and then the SUV heads toward the highway, with Gabriel in trail at a safe remove. About fifteen miles outside the city, Gabriel sees the SUV exit the highway and pull off onto a dirt road.

Gabriel exits as well but stops after going only a few yards down the dirt road. He debates calling for some backup, but after contemplating his options for a few moments, he decides to go against his better judgment and continue down the road. As the path bends around a giant mound of bulldozed dirt that forms a makeshift wall, he sees a group of parked vehicles. He slows the truck and assesses the situation.

He can see that a line of men has formed near a white utility van. He parks his truck toward the back of the collection of vehicles. As he cuts the engine, he removes his badge and holster and places them in the glove compartment. He checks his handgun and ensures that there is a round in the chamber, but pauses, staring at it. "What if they frisk me?" he mutters aloud. After a slight hesitation, he decides to put the gun back in its holster, then tucks it away in the glove compartment.

He gets out of the truck and leaves the door slightly ajar, in case he needs to make a run for it. As he weaves between the trucks and cars on his way toward the van, it suddenly dawns on him that he is too clean; the line is full of day laborers and migrant workers. He stops and squats down. Grabbing handfuls of earth, he rigorously rubs the dirt into his forearms and face. Figuring he shouldn't overdo it, he rubs the remaining residue on his white shirt. As he approaches the back of the makeshift line, he can see a tall, lean man with a very muscular build walking in circles, intently staring at different parts of the ground. Men who were previously prone on the ground stand up and adjust their belts after pulling their pants up from around their ankles.

The line starts moving. He is now third from the front. He can hear the negotiations taking place between the lead man and a much shorter man in a Hawaiian shirt.

"For twenty dollars, I get the ass *and* pussy?" Gabriel hears the man at the front of the line ask.

"*Mano*, if you give me twenty dollars, I don't care what hole you stick it in," the salesman sighs; he is clearly worn out and ready to pack it in.

The man fishes a wad of cash out of his pocket and begins to count it. Annoyed at his lack of preparedness, and upon hearing a bell ring, the salesman points to the man in second place and asks, "Hey, pussy or ass?"

The man is quick, a ten-dollar bill already in hand as he moves forward. "Pussy!"

Angry, the man in first place tries to interfere with the break in order by putting his arm out, recklessly attempting to shove the salesman back so he can't accept the second man's money. In the blink of an eye, the salesman has his gun drawn. "Don't you *fucking* do that, bitch. Everyone, back up!"

Gabriel's heart races with adrenaline at the scene playing out before him; he wants to step in, but he keeps his wits about him and does what he is told, moving a step back with the rest of the line.

At this point, the tall man who was walking the perimeter has entered the fray. As Gabriel stands submissively, his hands in the air, he watches the salesman and his partner beat the man until he is nearly dead. When the man goes limp, showing not so much as a twitch, the salesman reaches down and picks up the money that the offender dropped. He pockets it, then delivers a final, half-hearted kick to the man's ribs.

The tall partner stands to his full height and addresses the now muddled line. "If any of you fucking bitches try that shit, I will fucking gut you," he yells, pulling a knife from his belt and holding it up for all to see.

As the partner walks back to resume his rounds, the salesman looks at Gabriel. "OK, man, what do you want?" When Gabriel doesn't respond right away, still staring after the partner, the salesman snaps his fingers in Gabriel's face. "Hey! Pussy or ass? I don't got all day."

Finally focusing on the salesman, Gabriel mutters an, "Oh, yeah," and shoves his hand into his pocket. He pulls out a twenty-dollar bill and holds it out to the salesman but remains silent.

"Motherfucker, I'm not making change for you, so you're getting the ass." The salesman snatches the money out of his hand and points the federal agent toward an available woman.

As Gabriel passes him and heads toward the woman, the salesman smacks his lips together, making a kissing sound at his partner. The partner looks back and signals with his hand that he caught the sound; Gabriel realizes this is a code between the two men to indicate who has paid for anal sex.

Gabriel approaches his designated spot and sees a scattering of women and men engaged in various stages of bought intercourse. He finds the woman that he has been assigned to, and gets on his knees as he begins to unbuckle his belt. Gabriel slides himself between the woman's legs, with his pants only slightly pulled down; he has no intention on having sex with this woman.

He doesn't realize that the tall partner is standing behind him, watching Gabriel's every move—or, in this case, lack of moves.

"What the fuck are you doing, *mano*? You paid for the ass," the man says as he kicks Gabriel's foot. As he walks around them to move on, he looks down and sees that the girl has forgotten to start her timer. The man kicks some dirt in the woman's face and says, "Start the timer, you stupid bitch." As he walks away, he adds, "And turn over, he paid for your dirty ass."

Gabriel looks to his left and watches the man continue his rounds. As the woman underneath him quickly rolls over, Gabriel finds himself filled with rage. For a few minutes, Gabriel pretends to thrust into the woman. The woman lays resting the side of her face on the carpet, baffled, but nonetheless happy that she has been granted a break from her usual misery. A few minutes pass, but before her bell can ring, Gabriel dismounts and adjusts his pants. The woman slightly raises on her forearm and looks at him over her shoulder, confused, but he ignores her.

As he leaves, he passes the long line of men at the van and continues his brisk pace until he reaches his truck. Once inside, he opens the glove compartment. He stares at his gun, itching to go back over and kill both pimps and any john that gets in his way. It takes everything he has to stop himself, but after a moment, he starts the engine and heads back toward the highway.

CHAPTER NINE
THE SPA

Located just a few miles southwest of The Galleria is the world famous "Spa of Houston." In business since 1986, this spa is one of Houston's oldest and most beloved brothels. Hobbyists refer to it on various escort rating websites as a "must see location for all out-of-towners." The spa is known for its beautiful women and clean rooms. It's not that the police don't know about it...they do. They just respect the fact that the proprietors never have any drama, and they pay their taxes. "Taxes," in this case, mean bribes to the right city officials. The spa isn't located near any schools or any residential areas; it is quietly tucked away between a small scrap metal yard and an old used records store. It attracts a more upscale clientele than the fields do. These clients require the kind of discretion that the cartels offer. In over twenty years, the spa hasn't been raided by the police nor robbed by any street-level gangs. Hector Ramirez is the spa "manager," for lack of a better term. Those who can see it for what it really is would call him a pimp.

Rodrigo stands with Rosalie at the back entrance to the spa, waiting for Hector to let them in. Impatient, Rodrigo jams his finger into the button to ring the bell again.

At last, a white woman in a string bikini answers the door. She looks irritated, and silently steps aside to hold the door open for them. As Rodrigo and Rosalie enter the establishment, the white woman looks Rosalie up and down as a gladiator would look at another competitor in the Colosseum.

Inside, they are struck by the crisp air; the building feels as cold as the arctic circle. The woman leads them to a small "break room" of sorts, where two other women are sitting at a small card table. One woman is eating a cup of microwave ramen noodles, and the other is reading a cheap gossip magazine. Both women are wearing large sweaters. The white woman from the entrance removes a similar heavy sweater from a coat rack and begins to put it on. Just as she gets it over her head, a doorbell sounds from the front of the building. The white woman stops mid-motion, then pulls the sweater back off her head and puts it back on the rack, huffing in irritation.

The two women from the card table rise and remove their sweaters as well, revealing that they too are wearing string bikinis that barely cover their private parts. The three women exit the break room and walk carefully in their high heels down the central hall to the front of the building.

On a black and white monitor in the break room, Rodrigo watches a tall black man standing inside a waiting area near the front as he speaks to the women. There is no audio on the monitor, but through the hallway, Rodrigo can faintly hear the interactions taking place between the trio of ladies and the prospective client. A few moments pass and the man can be seen exiting through the front door. From a second black and white monitor, Rodrigo watches the man get in his car and drive away. This second monitor time shares between cameras on all sides of the exterior of the building. As it automatically switches, it shows the van in the back parking lot.

The three women return to the break room. The white woman snatches her sweater off the wall and tugs it on. In a thick southern accent, she says, "Fuckin' black guys are always window shopping. Shit's fuckin' pissing me off. I'm not going out there the next time I see a black guy come in. Fuck that noise."

Rodrigo wants to bash her head in, but checks the impulse. This isn't the field, and he isn't in charge here.

One of the other women, a skinny black woman in her early twenties, agrees. "Shit, next time a black guy comes in, I ain't goin' out there neither. They never pick me, anyway. They just want you bird-shit bitches and fucking Mexicans." She scoffs as she goes back to her magazine. "Shit, they just check the line-up and then go to fuck the Asian bitches down the way."

The third girl, a Hispanic woman with long, thick hair, jumps into the conversation. "You better not let Hector hear you saying that shit. Last time I didn't go out for line up, he taxed the shit outta me. I was just in the bathroom and he still took money from me."

The two other women blow her off, as if that couldn't happen to them. The white woman opens her mouth to say something, but a door across the hall opens, and the final sounds of a toilet flushing fill the silence instead.

"Rodrigo! How are you doing, man? It's been a long time," Hector says as he emerges from the bathroom. As they shake hands, Hector pulls Rodrigo in for a brotherly hug that makes Rodrigo nervous.

Rodrigo takes a small step back, putting distance between himself and Hector. "Yeah, it's been a while. I can't wait for you to teach me how to run a place like this. With nice air conditioning and shit."

Hector grins as he says, "Be patient, man, your time will come. I did my time in that hot fucking sun too, so don't worry. It gets better."

Before he can reply, Rodrigo's phone goes off in his pocket, again. He checks it and sees that it is Alger, who has been calling him incessantly. "Ahh, shit, I have to go. Alger is out back and we have to go to the spot."

"No problem, man." Hector gestures for Rodrigo to head to the door.

As Hector walks Rodrigo out, Rodrigo says, "The next time we get a really pretty one, we will bring her to you first. Luis says it's a waste to sell the sexy ones for ten dollars a fuck."

Hector laughs and shakes his head. "No, *mano*. You have to make them do a few days in the field so they appreciate this place. They have to see Hell before they can appreciate Heaven," he says, spreading his arms wide.

Rodrigo smirks and exits toward the van.

Inside the break room, Rosalie stares at the black and white monitor, watching Rodrigo get in the passenger side of the van and drive away. Even though she dislikes him, he has become familiar to her, and anxiety begins to creep in now that he is gone. She doesn't know what to make of this new situation, or of Hector; she was surprised to see Rodrigo acting submissive, when normally he is so commanding. She fidgets, pulling at a loose thread on her dress as she waits for Hector to return.

When Hector rejoins the women, he introduces himself. Rosalie isn't disarmed by his kind demeanor. Since she was taken from her home, the people that have been nicest to her have often been the most evil. She remains silent but nods politely to him.

The other Hispanic girl is introduced as Zoe, the black girl as Juicy, and finally the white girl as Paris. Hector explains that the girls have been given stage names to make them seem more playful to the clients. However, he says that Rosalie is such a good name that she will keep it as her stage name. Rosalie doesn't quite understand this concept, since she has never communicated with any of her "clients," so she just nods again as if she understands.

Hector takes her on a tour of the facility. He walks her down to the front of the hall. Before her stands a metal gate in a reinforced steel frame. It is allegedly impregnable and separates the prospective clients from the "models" as the men decide who they want to give them a private show. Once the client chooses a model, he pays the room fee of sixty dollars. The model then buzzes him inside and grants him access to the hallway.

As Hector shows her the "modeling studios," he takes care to be thorough in showing her where all the panic buttons are located in each room. He also points out a pinhole camera above each door. Rosalie is baffled at the idea of protections being in place for her safety; the spa is a far cry from the field.

Though Rosalie has never seen a spa before, the rooms look as she would expect, even going so far as to have a massage table in each. However, she begins to notice that everything is in various stages of disrepair. From the stained carpet to the rips in the upholstery, the whole place reeks of a phony business. Authenticity is not required; the basic gist of a legitimate business is all that matters.

Hector sits on a massage table in one of the rooms and goes over the fees for each service, which he refers to as her "tips." For a hand job, she is to charge forty dollars. Oral sex, one hundred dollars. Vaginal sex costs one hundred and forty dollars, and anal sex costs an even two hundred.

"You gotta try and push for full service at all times. See, the business won't be very profitable if we're just selling hand jobs. So, upsell. Try to get them to go all the way."

Still a novice in the world of sex, she stares at Hector, bewildered. He laughs to himself and reassures her that she will learn as she goes. Then he drops a tidbit of interesting information on her: She will keep twenty-five percent of her "tips."

With her head still spinning from the impromptu class, he takes her back to the break room. Zoe and Juicy are still sitting at the card table, both flipping through magazines. Paris has decided to take a nap on a small couch.

"Alright, take off that horrible dress." Hector says as he begins rummaging through a small drawer of bikini tops and bottoms. Rosalie is already starting to shiver from the cold air but does as she is told. As she stands naked, Hector continues to search the stuffed drawer for the smallest bikini possible—the smaller, the better. Finally, he grabs both a top and bottom and closes the drawer. As he holds the mismatched bikini in his hands, he turns and looks at Rosalie. As his eyes scan her body, they stop at her unkempt pubic hair and he scowls. "Damn it. They didn't shave you."

Frustrated, he barks, "Zoe, take her and show her how to trim her pussy."

Zoe reluctantly gets up and grabs a pair of scissors from a shelf. "Come on, *chica*," says Zoe as she playfully snips the scissors. She leads Rosalie to one of the modeling rooms and lays a small towel on the table. Zoe pats the spot with the towel and tells Rosalie to sit there. Rosalie hesitates, her eyes darting to the scissors in Zoe's hand, but does as she is told.

Zoe grabs a stool from the corner of the room and sits eye-level with Rosalie's waist. "Relax, I'm not going to hurt you," says Zoe in Spanish as she spreads Rosalie's legs and positions herself between them. When Rosalie remains tense and timid, Zoe sighs and asks, "Where are you from?"

Watching every movement of Zoe's hands as she begins to trim her pubic hair, Rosalie says, "Mexico."

Zoe giggles, pulling her hand back for a moment so she can look up at Rosalie. "I know Mexico, silly. Where in Mexico?"

"Cochoapa el Grande."

Zoe can sense Rosalie's uncertainty about what's going on. "Look. You are as lucky as you are going to get by being here," she gestures with the scissors to mean the Spa, "so don't mess it up."

Rosalie frowns, her brow furrowing. "What do you mean?"

"Just keep to yourself, get the men to *love* you, and *don't* piss off Hector. He is a pretty good man. He doesn't make us fuck him, cuz he's gay and shit. He looks out for us. He says he doesn't make us do anything that he hasn't done himself," says Zoe with a slight giggle at the end.

After a moment, Rosalie asks, "Will I get to leave here?"

"Well...I can come and go as I please because I'm an American like Juicy and Paris. I just work here for the money. You girls can buy your freedom with your money, eventually. Hector keeps it for you so thieves like Paris don't steal it. Don't worry, though, us Mexican girls make the most money here. All these white guys want us brown girls." Zoe winks and playfully slaps Rosalie on the thigh, as if the two of them share a bond because of their Mexican heritage.

Zoe's comments cause Rosalie to flash back to Cúcuy, to the first time she was raped. The image of Cucuy standing over her afterwards, still etched into her mind with vivid clarity, sends a chill through her body.

"Ahh, careful, *chica*...try to stay still. You don't want me to snip your *chocha*," she says playfully, as Rosalie nervously fidgets. "There. That should do it. These white guys don't want a shaved *chocha*. They just want it clean and tidy."

She motions for Rosalie to get up, then carefully folds the towel and picks it up so that none of the clipped hair falls on the floor. As they walk down the hall toward the back door, Zoe playfully swats Rosalie on her butt. "Aye, *chica*, put on your bottoms. You don't want to give a free show."

Rosalie begins to put on the bikini bottom, but while trying to keep pace in trail of Zoe, she can only get one leg though with every couple of steps. As she finally pulls the bikini bottom up, Zoe opens the back door and begins to wave the towel, releasing the hair clippings off into the wind. Rosalie looks on in awe that the other woman has such liberties.

Back in the break room, Rosalie stands awkwardly, looking to Zoe for a cue as to what she should do; she has begun to think of Zoe as her guardian.

Zoe notices this and motions for her to sit down on a small recliner. As Zoe searches through a tall locker in the corner, she says, "You can have this. I always keep an extra layer. Hector keeps it so fucking cold in here because he thinks the johns like to escape from the heat outside."

Rosalie catches the old zip-up sweater Zoe tosses her, and for the first time in as long as she can remember, Rosalie smiles. She puts the sweater on and zips it up, happy for some reprieve from the cold. As she sinks back into the soft recliner, she thinks that things might finally be alright.

A doorbell sounds, and the three veterans begin to strip off their sweaters and walk toward the front lobby. Rosalie begins to rise, but as Zoe exits the room, she tells her, "Aye, *chica*, don't worry about this one. Just stay here and rest."

Rosalie revels in the opportunity to sleep comfortably and sits back to watch the monitor. She sees what looks like a white man in his mid-twenties playfully bantering with the three ladies as they vie for his affection. The man chooses Zoe and slides money through a slot in the gate. Moments later, Juicy and Paris return to the break room, annoyed that they were not selected.

Zoe takes the man to a modeling room and leaves him there alone with the door shut, to "get comfortable."

Zoe walks back into the break room as Hector exits his small office in the adjacent room. "Who's up for the guy in room three?" he asks to no one in particular.

As Zoe picks up a portable plastic shower caddy filled with various items, she glances at him. "Me." She hands the sixty dollars to Hector, then tries to exit the room to return to her customer, but Hector stops her and looks at Rosalie.

"Take her with you. Show her how the session is supposed to work. He didn't pay for her, so you do all the fucking."

Zoe frowns as she looks down at Rosalie and heaves a heavy sigh. "Come on, *chica*, and take that sweater off."

As Rosalie moves to follow Zoe into the hallway, Hector grabs her by the arm. "You don't miss lineups—EVER! You aren't here to just sit around." Hector releases his grip, allowing the two bikini-clad women to walk down the hallway to a room marked "3."

Before entering, Zoe hands the caddy to Rosalie. With both hands now free, Zoe fluffs up her hair and grabs a spray bottle from the caddy. It is mouthwash, and she sprays some in her mouth. She looks at Rosalie and says, "Trust me, honey, you need some too," as she points the sprayer at Rosalie's lips.

Rosalie opens her mouth, grimacing when she feels the cool sting of the mouthwash as its spray hits her tongue. Rosalie looks down at the other contents of the tray. A small roll of paper towels, a pack of baby wipes, a spray bottle of rubbing alcohol, and a bottle of massage oil are carefully organized in the caddy.

Zoe opens the door, and Rosalie follows her into the room. Inside, the man is already naked, with a towel covering his lap as he sits on the edge of the massage table. Zoe locks the door as she closes it, and Rosalie finds herself on edge again upon hearing the *click*.

The man is startled to see two women when he was only expecting one. "Hey, what is this? Who is she?" the man asks as his eyes nervously dart between them.

"Don't worry, *papi*. She's a new girl. I gotta show her the ropes," says Zoe in an attempt to calm the man down.

The man isn't buying it; he suspects it's some sort of trap set up by the police to catch him in the act. "No way. This doesn't feel right. I'm outta here." Already, he is attempting to put his pants back on.

Thinking very quickly, Zoe grabs one of Rosalie's breasts and pulls the top down to reveal her nipple. "Come on, *papi*. This place is legit. If she was a cop, you think she would let me show you her titty?"

This calms the man, but he is still skeptical. Seeing that he is still not convinced, Zoe moves her hand further down and pulls the front of Rosalie's bikini bottom to the side, showing the man her vagina. The man puts his pants back down on a small chair. "OK, so what do you want?" asks Zoe.

"Full service," replies the man.

"Full service, back door? Or just regular full service?"

"Just regular full service," the man says, and Rosalie is surprised to see he almost looks embarrassed.

"OK, that's one-forty, *papi*," Zoe informs him casually as she grabs the shower caddy from Rosalie and places it on a small table along the wall.

The man picks up his pants and reaches into one of the pockets. He pulls out a wad of seven crisp twenty-dollar bills already folded together. Without counting the money, he places it on the table next to the shower caddy. Zoe picks up the bankroll and begins to count it carefully. When she is satisfied, she places the money back on the table and walks toward the man.

Zoe begins to softly caress the man with one hand as she removes her top with the other. Once her top is off, the man takes her breasts in both hand and squeezes them. She gently pushes the man onto the massage table and instructs him to lay on his back. To

Rosalie, she says, "Go on the other side and watch. I'll show you how to do this right."

Rosalie walks to the other side of the table but keeps her eyes on the floor. She doesn't want to see; it feels like a violation, though to her or to Zoe, she can't tell.

"*Chica*, you have to learn," Zoe tells her softly.

Taking a deep breath, Rosalie looks up and watches as Zoe removes an unopened condom that was tucked into the front of her bikini bottom. As she unwraps it, the man says, "I was hoping for a bareback blow job."

Zoe empathetically exhales and says, "Ohh, I'm sorry, *papi*. We don't do that here. We gotta worry about our health, no?"

Zoe places the condom against her lips, parting them slightly, and gently bites the tip on the condom. Bending over at the waist, she uses her mouth to unroll the condom over his now fully erect shaft. The man puts his right hand on Zoe's head and begins to breathe deeply, in and out. Slowly, he brings his left hand over toward Rosalie and squeezes her butt.

Zoe, upon noticing this, immediately stops what she is doing and stands straight up. Seductively, she says, "No, sir...you did not pay for that. You paid for this." She pushes down her bikini bottom and lets it slide down her legs to the floor.

The man removes his hand from Rosalie, and she notices a gleam in his eye like that of Cucuy as he asks, "How much extra for the two of you?"

Still wearing her high heels, Zoe climbs atop the table and straddles the man. "Ahh, *papi*, am I not enough for you?"

As Zoe begins to rock her hips to and fro, the man forgets all about Rosalie, and she backs away. The man grabs Zoe's hips, guiding her to thrust faster until he quickly climaxes. Zoe allows the man to stop spasming and then climbs off, careful to make sure she doesn't inadvertently pull the condom off.

Zoe walks to the caddy and removes a few baby wipes from their container. After she spends a few moments using them to clean her crotch, she rips off a paper towel and wraps it around the used wipes. She rips another paper towel from the roll and grabs a few more baby wipes, then returns to the man. He lies motionless, his eyes closed, still overpowered with euphoria. She uses the paper towel to gently remove the condom from the man's penis, all the while careful not to spill a drop. She wads up the towel and sets it to the side, then uses the baby wipes to clean his crotch and asks him if he wants some rubbing alcohol.

The man, coming out of his daze, has only one thought in his mind: Get the fuck out of here. With a curt shake of his head, he says, "NO," and practically jumps off the table to put his clothes back on.

Zoe quickly puts her bikini back on as the man dresses. In a flash, he is standing by the door, ready to leave. His arms folded across his chest, he appears restless and impatient as he waits to be released. With her bikini slightly askew, Zoe unlocks the door and walks the man to the interior steel gate that leads to the waiting area. As soon as the gate is open, the man rushes out, flies through the front door, and promptly gets in his car.

84

Zoe returns to the room to find Rosalie standing in the doorway. "That's how it is. They can't wait to get in here, then they can't wait to get out." She rolls her eyes, then looks at Rosalie sternly. "Remember, *chica*: YOU are in charge in this room. Nothing happens that they don't pay for."

Zoe walks past Rosalie, back over to the caddy, and pulls her bikini bottom to the side. She sprays her vagina with the rubbing alcohol, wincing as it stings her tender flesh, then grabs a paper towel to dry her crotch. As she does this, she says, "Notice how I kept calling him *papi*? White boys love that shit. Gets them to cum quick. Really lay on that Mexican accent when you do it."

Rosalie nods as she watches Zoe. "What are you doing?"

Finishing up her cleaning ritual, Zoe looks at her with wide, serious eyes. "*Chica*, you gotta keep yourself clean. You don't want to catch something off one of these pigs."

Zoe rips off a final wad of four paper towels and grabs all the trash that was produced from the session. She motions for Rosalie to pick up the caddy, then surveys the room one last time. Satisfied that it is as clean as it was before, Zoe and Rosalie exit the room and Zoe turns the lights out. The room is ready for its next customer.

CHAPTER TEN
THE SHOOTOUT

"I sure hope these guys come out here every day, or else this is gonna be one big waste of time," says Special Agent Uribe.

"They'll be here. This is a cash cow for these guys," Gabriel assures him, still angry over the cruelty he witnessed during his solo surveillance. "They'll be here."

The two men lay prone in a small clearing about four hundred yards away from the field that the carpet ladies work. They are both wearing Kevlar vests, in addition to other tactical gear. An M4 assault rifle lies next to Gabriel, along with several bottles of water.

Uribe observes from his binoculars an old jalopy parked near the area in question. The vehicle's only occupant waits patiently as he taps a beat with his hands on the steering wheel. "Maybe they take Monday's off; maybe, like this guy, we just didn't get the memo."

Gabriel, surveying the dirt road, responds, "Nahh, he's just an eager beaver. They probably only come closer to dusk, when it's a little cooler and everybody is done working."

Uribe sighs. "I wish we could have taken a few days to surveil their setup and maybe follow them back to where they keep the girls."

Gabriel hasn't been completely forthcoming with his supervisor. He fears the retribution he may face for paying the pimps money to dry hump a sex slave. His reconnaissance of the criminal activity reported that he only observed the setup from a distance, based on information gleaned from his gardener. It's for this reason that he asked to not be a part of the two tactical teams that keep driving in circles on the highway, never more than a half-mile from the dirt road exit.

Gabriel lowers his binoculars and looks at Uribe, hoping to appeal to his sense of reason. "Dave, you know these women are being kept in a fucking basement somewhere. They don't have a couple days for us to watch as they get raped over and over again. Besides, what if they change it up? They were gone by the time we got back yesterday. We don't even know that they are gonna come back here. If they do show up, we gotta hit them now, out in the open, where no innocent bystanders are in the way."

Over their handheld radio, the pilot of the Cessna 206 Stationair, which has been circling three thousand feet overhead, comes through: "We have a white utility van exiting I-10. It's headed down the dirt path and approaching the field."

Uribe and Gabriel look to their left and see the van in question driving down the dirt road. The van leaves their view for a few moments as it passes behind the giant mound of dirt that forms a wall between the freeway and the field.

"Copy that. We have eyes on the van. TAC one and TAC two, stay in your holding pattern. Let's wait till they're set up," Agent Uribe orders over the radio.

Over the radio's speaker, they can hear Teresa acknowledging the order. Shortly after, Agent Bennett acknowledges from TAC two.

The van parks and two men exit. The man in the jalopy exits his vehicle as well, hoping to be first in line. As the driver of the van closes his door, he holds his hand up and orders the man to wait by his car.

From Uribe's peripheral view, he notices a few more vehicles exit the highway and bend around the dirt path. "Fuck me. What did they do? Send out a fucking mass text saying, 'We're open for business'?"

Through his binoculars, Gabriel watches as the two pimps open the back of the van and order the women out. Seven women exit, each with a small piece of carpet, as the taller pimp quickly points out where each girl is to set up. In their haste, they forget to pass out the egg timers. The fatter pimp runs quickly from girl to girl, tossing an egg timer at each one. By the time he returns to the van with his empty bag, a line of five men has formed, and more vehicles continue to arrive.

With every woman now occupied, Uribe radios for the TAC teams to post up at the freeway exit. Then, he watches as, worn out from the sweltering heat, the taller pimp stands at the far end of the circle of women, resting his forearms on the top of his head.

Nine vehicles in total have arrived. "Shit, I didn't think we'd be dealing with this many guys, not this quickly," says Uribe.

"Eh, I bet when shit pops off, most of the johns will—" Gabriel is cut off by the sound of gunfire. Three men, all previously standing in the line, have drawn handguns and are in the process of robbing the two pimps. They got the drop on the salesman by shooting him in the head, killing him instantly.

The pimp walking the perimeter returns fire toward the van. One of the assailants continues rifling through the dead pimp's cargo pockets, covered by his partners, and retreats only after he steals a large wad of cash. From the wall of bullets coming from the two other robbers, the tall pimp is hit in the shoulder and falls to the ground. The three men run toward their red SUV; they climb in quickly and drive toward the freeway.

By this time, many of the johns have gotten in their vehicles and are also attempting to flee the area. As the events were quickly unfolding, Agent Uribe was quarterbacking the response of the two TAC teams at the entrance to the dirt road. "RED SUV, RED SUV. THREE MEN IN THE RED SUV. ALL ARMED. THEY JUST ROBBED AND KILLED THE PIMPS. DON'T WORRY ABOUT THE OTHER VEHICLES. TAKE THE RED SUV!" Uribe screams into the radio.

From their vantage point, Gabriel and Uribe can see the two Suburbans, full of agents, drive forward around the bend in the road. From the other side of the dirt wall, the red SUV drives recklessly as it tries to avoid the other exiting vehicles.

Gabriel jumps to his feet and grabs his assault rifle, then runs as fast as he can toward the hill. A much more out of shape Uribe follows. As Uribe runs, he looks to his right and sees that the men previously on top of the women have all scattered into the distance, running in the opposite direction of the freeway. Some of the women have sat up on their carpets, and almost look like moles popping their heads up out of the dirt.

Automatic gunfire rings out from the other side of the mound. Uribe attempts to get a report over the radio but with no success. More shots are fired, this time more rapid, and concentrated. Teresa's voice blasts from the radio: "DRIVERS DOWN! DRIVERS DOWN!"

Then, Agent Bennett comes through: "I think the front side passenger is down. The third guy is around the back side."

More gunfire erupts. "AGENT DOWN! AGENT DOWN! CALL EMS!" shouts a male voice over the radio.

His heart pounding, Gabriel is almost to the wall of dirt and attempts to move around to what he believes is the rear of the red SUV's position. Teresa's voice breaks through the static again: "HE'S RUNNING! DAMNIT, I DON'T HAVE A SHOT! HE'S DUCKING BEHIND…"

Just then, the man suddenly appears from the other side. With quick reflexes, Gabriel lifts his rifle and fires two rounds into the man's chest. As he walks up to assess the man's condition, he decides to put another round in the man's head. This Mozambique Drill will be frowned upon by the shooting board, but *they* aren't out here, in the heat of battle.

Uribe sees that Gabriel has neutralized his threat and relays to the other agents that the man is down.

"Roger. The driver's dead too. We have the front passenger in custody." The radio fills with static for a moment as Teresa hesitates. When her voice comes through again, it is quiet. "Louis is down...he's dead."

Uribe and Gabriel lock eyes across the field, both shocked. Moving fast, Uribe jogs over and rounds the makeshift dirt wall. Two agents stand over Agent Bennett's body, and Teresa is crouching next to him. Uribe pushes his way through and looks at the scene.

"Damn," Uribe sighs. Bennett was wearing his Kevlar vest, but a bullet struck him in the neck and passed through his spine. "At least he went painlessly."

Uribe rubs his hands roughly down his face, taking a second to regroup, then looks up and orders Gabriel and the two male agents standing over Bennett's body to go down to the van and round up the girls.

All three men ignore the order. Staring at their fallen brother, they are all still in shock. Gabriel feels the weight of his death more than the others, as he feels partially responsible.

"GO!" Uribe barks. "NOW, GODDAMN IT!"

As the men finally move, Teresa remains with her fallen comrade. "You did good, new guy," she murmurs as she carefully removes his gun from his lifeless hand. The ballistics report will later reveal that, of the forty-two bullets fired at the red SUV, it was one of Agent Louis Bennett's that struck and killed the driver.

Gabriel and the two other agents approach the van on foot and carefully take note of the dead pimp that the three men robbed. Gabriel reaches down and checks for a pulse. When he finds none, he removes the gun from the dead man's holster and unloads it.

Teresa has joined the men. Wanting to make sure the women are not injured, she says, "You check the van, and I'll check the girls."

While Gabriel walks around the back of the van, the other agents follow Teresa. As they make their way to the women, one of the agents comments on how surprised he is that none of the women tried to make a run for it.

"Too dumb to realize they could have gotten away," scoffs the other.

Teresa stops cold and whips around to face the agent. "Where the fuck would they have gone?" she barks. Both agents have the good grace to at least look chastised. They walk on silently.

Teresa surveys the women and deems them unscathed—or at least free of bullet wounds. She gives the go-ahead to start rounding them up, but as the men collect the women and attempt to move them back toward the van, they hear a moan.

"HANDS! SHOW ME YOUR HANDS!" shouts one of the agents; all three surround the injured pimp. As one agent snatches up the gun laying on the ground near the wounded man, the other aggressively flips him onto his stomach.

As the handcuffs are snapped on his wrists, he finally speaks: "Did they kill my friend?"

Teresa squats next to his head. "Yeah, they blew his fucking head off. I wouldn't worry about that if I was you, though. I'd be worrying about the class two felony that you're about to eat."

The two male agents lift the pimp to his feet and one asks Teresa sarcastically, "Hey, in Texas that's up to twenty years in prison, right?"

Now standing face to face with the pimp, Teresa looks up at the much taller man. "Twenty years...per count. Seven times twenty equals what, *puto*?" she spits the question, then answers for him: "That's a hundred and forty years." Stepping back, she laughs sardonically, and lays her Mexican accent on thick when she says, "A man as pretty as you is gonna have a rough time there."

The pimp looks at her stone-faced. "Now that I'm your prisoner, don't you have to give me medical attention?"

Teresa simply nods for the other agents to take him away. As he is escorted away by the two men, Teresa remains behind. With her hands on her hips, she looks around and can't help but feel overwhelmed by the day's events. Thinking no one is looking at her, she brings both hands up to cover her face and takes a deep breath, but it's no use. As the tears begin to fall, she sinks to the ground. Just as the first full sob overtakes her, she hears a voice: "Don't cry. Everything will be alright."

Her hands fall to her lap as she looks around for the voice's owner, and she sees a slightly chubby girl, now sitting up on one of the carpets. Teresa smiles at the girl and climbs to her feet, wiping her face with the heels of her hands. She walks over to the girl and helps her off the carpet, and as they walk toward the van, Teresa puts her arm around the former carpet lady and says, "Thank You".

CHAPTER ELEVEN
THE INTERROGATION

Standing in front of the observation side of a two-way mirror, Gabriel and Special Agent Uribe stare quietly at the man on the other side. Bandaged up but appearing no worse for the wear is the tall pimp from the shootout: Rodrigo Washington.

Teresa enters the room. "So, how are you gonna play this guy?" she asks Gabriel.

"How are *you* gonna play this guy, Teresa? You're gonna go in there and question him." Worried that, on the off chance Rodrigo remembers him, he could get jammed up, Gabriel suggested Teresa do this interrogation. He is already going to be in hot water for putting a bullet in the one robber's head execution style; he doesn't need to risk opening up another can of worms.

Teresa stares at the men, wide-eyed and more than a little nervous—this will be her first solo interrogation.

At her reaction, Uribe gives her a good-natured slap on the shoulder and says, "We talked it over and we think you're ready for this."

"Remember, don't let him feel like he's in charge. If you think he's getting the upper hand, just remind him that he's gonna get ass raped in prison. That normally knocks them down a peg or two," Gabriel advises.

Teresa inhales deeply and then blows the breath out in a whoosh before turning on her heel and exiting the room. Just as she is about to close the door, Gabriel calls, "Ohh, Ter."

Teresa looks back toward Gabriel over her shoulder, an eyebrow raised. He tells her, "Don't hit him," and she smiles as she closes the door.

The two men watch her through the glass as she enters the interrogation room.

Teresa casually drops a thick file folder on the table and takes a seat across from the prisoner. "Rodrigo Washington," she addresses him, taking care to emphasize his last name with an overly American pronunciation. "How'd you get a handle like that?"

He taps his finger against the edge of the table, appearing bored. "My mother thought having an American-sounding name would help me in this country."

"Ahh, that's right. You're an Anchor Baby. Your mom just swam across the Rio Grande and shit you right on out, huh? Then you became *our* problem. Well, I gotta tell you, with how things are going at the border, you were gonna become our problem one way or another." She shrugs. "I digress. So, how long you been running the girls for?"

"I don't know what you are talking about. I got lost in a field and three guys started shooting at me. I saw a gun on the ground, so I picked it up. I had to defend myself...right?" replies Rodrigo coolly.

"That's the bullshit story you're gonna go with? Really?" She raises her eyebrows at him, shaking her head and blowing air through lips. "If that's the best story that you can come up with, you are dumber than you look...and you look pretty fucking stupid."

She was hoping to get a rise out of him, but sees not even the faintest crack in his relaxed demeanor.

She leans in and half whispers to him, as if she has a secret to tell him, "Come on, aren't you pissed that those three *pendejos* iced your friend...and you couldn't even kill one of them?"

Finally, she spies a muscle twitch in his jaw, but he simply leans forward and whispers back, "Didn't it take like ten of you *federales* to kill those three *pendejos*...but not before they got one of your friends, too?"

Teresa doesn't hide her emotion as well as Rodrigo; she wears her hatred on her face for the whole world to see.

In the other room, Uribe mutters, "Come on, Velazquez, don't let him get to you. This isn't a movie; focus on the facts."

Teresa rolls her neck, slowly regaining her composure. "So, how much were you selling pussy for out there? Thirty bucks? More? Less?"

"I've never sold any pussy before, but I heard the other guys talking, and I think they were paying ten for pussy and twenty for the ass." Rodrigo blinks wide eyes at her, still feigning innocence.

"Twenty dollars. Wow! To think, your sweet ass will be going for as little as ten cigarettes over in Beaumont." Getting her rhythm back, she leans back in her chair and folds her hands behind her head, making a show of looking him over. "Those pretty eyes...good bone structure...overall *cunty* face...Yes, sir, at United States Penitentiary Beaumont...you're a ten."

"I don't know about no one hundred and forty years, like you said before. In Texas, it's not illegal for me to own a gun. In this state, people are encouraged to defend not only themselves, but others too. I saw three men shooting at a field full of women. I had to protect them. Those poor women needed me, and I tried my best," says Rodrigo as he slams his hand dramatically on the metal table.

Crossing her arms over her chest, she laughs. "Already, you are changing your story. I thought you found the gun, no?" In a flash, she stands, her hands splayed on the table as she yells, "You are going to prison for making those women slaves. You forced them to have sex with strangers for money."

Rodrigo scoffs. "Did you see me take any money? No? Did you see me tell the women to fuck those guys? *No.* I ain't afraid of you charging me with shit, because I didn't do shit."

There's a sudden knock on the glass, alerting Teresa that she needs to wrap it up. "You deserve an academy award, you piece of shit. Don't worry, I'll be right back."

As she leaves the interrogation room, Rodrigo says, "Don't worry, I'll be right here," and smacks his lips at her.

Inside the observation room, she sees that Gabriel has left and Uribe has been joined by the State's Attorney.

"Teresa, this is State's Attorney Ross here," says Uribe.

She acknowledges him, then looks intensely at Uribe as she asks, "What's going on, guys? This is fucking up my rhythm."

"Rhythm? It feels like I was watching a bad t.v. show just now. Jesus, Teresa, you know that's not how to run an interrogation. Stick to the facts. Don't overdo the whole 'prison rape' shit. You get any more aggressive in there and we risk a harassment investigation." Uribe rolls his eyes at Teresa, who is becoming more pissed off by the second. "Anyway, this is gonna fuck your quote-unquote *rhythm* up even more: We can't gig him for the human trafficking."

"What the hell? You have got to be kidding me! That guy is a fucking slave driver, and you guys are just gonna let him walk?"

"The best we can do is five years max for possessing a handgun with a serial number removed. We didn't see him take money, we didn't see him interact with any of the johns. The other guy handled the money," says the beaten and disappointed State's Attorney. "I'm sorry, we've got nothing."

"Look, Teresa, none of the girls are talking—they're too afraid. These guys did a real number on them. This fuck will make bail and we'll tail him after he gets released. Maybe he leads us back to the place where they house these girls, but my guess is, he'll just vanish." Uribe grabs a thin file folder off a table. Handing it to her, he says, "Look...Gabe is in room two with the shooter that you apprehended. Go in there and see what you two can get out of him. I'll take care of this fuck's processing on the weapons charge."

Resignation taking over in place of shock, Teresa makes her way to the second interrogation room, but stops just as she reaches for the handle and heads back to the room where Rodrigo still sits. She opens his door, but instead of entering, she simply stands in the doorway and says, "Why do you hate these girls so much? Was *tu madre* a whore on the other side? Is that it? Do you beat on the guys because they're like your father?" Rodrigo stares straight ahead, doing his best to ignore her. Before she leaves, she adds, "Remember my face, because you will be seeing me again, *puto*, I promise."

She closes the door and walks toward the second interrogation room, reading the file in her hand as she goes. As she walks in, she hears Gabriel mid-sentence: "Your ass is worth ten cigarettes, motherfucker."

Teresa closes the door and slaps the file on the table as she says, "Ballistics came back. The bullet that killed Agent Bennett came from your gun, *puto*. You know what that means? Huntsville...electric chair, motherfucker."

Gabriel continues off of her play, drawing out his words. "*Damn*, fucker. You're gonna be a sizzling little *vato,* aren't you? Kinda makes you wish you could go back to just getting pumped in the ass for life."

"Well," Teresa says, a sly smile creeping onto her face as she pretends to weigh some options, "we might be able to swing life in prison for you. That is, if you cooperate."

"I can't do no life in prison, man, come on. I didn't shoot that cop! Come on, man," the prisoner pleads, becoming frantic.

With faux tenderness, trying to soothe the man, Teresa says, "Baby, aww. Sweetheart, you're up for the electric chair. The only thing that can help you, is if you tell us about the men in the van."

Without even taking a moment to think, the man nods vehemently.

"So, you gonna tell us what we want to know?" asks Gabriel as he takes out a pen and sits down on the opposite side of the table.

"Yeah, just don't give me the electric chair, man," replies the frightened man.

Teresa pats his hand, lingering a second longer than necessary. "Baby, I promise you won't get the chair."

The man still looks skeptical but is reassured by Teresa's touch. "OK. I got the idea to rob these guys one day when I was waiting in line to get some pussy. I saw how much money they were making, so I told my friends that we should rob them. We started following them to figure out where they were staying."

"Where would they go?" asks Gabriel, pen at the ready.

"They would hop on I-10 and head to Baytown. A white two-story house. 116 Hacienda Lane."

Teresa cuts in to ask, "So they would go straight there at the end of every day?"

The prisoner slouches in his chair, beginning to relax as he talks. "No, not always. We followed them for almost a week. Every other day, they would stop at this one hotel and make the girls get out of the van."

Gabriel looks up from the pad of paper, his eyebrows raised. "So they were whoring the girls out of a hotel, too?"

"No, man. They were washing them," the man says, as if this is common knowledge. When Teresa and Gabriel exchange a glance, dumbfounded, he explains, "They would make them jump in the pool for a few minutes to kinda wash the stink off. I don't know...maybe it was like a treat for the girls. You know, after a hot day of work, to cool off."

Trying hard to rein in the disgust she feels, Teresa says, "Go on."

"Well, we noticed every other night a man in a black Mercedes would stop by."

"Describe him. What did he look like?" asks Gabriel.

"I don't know. He was, like, forty maybe, real skinny and wore tight shirts. We figured he was collecting the money, because he would walk up to the door and it would open before he even knocked or anything. The short man that Tito shot would hand the man a brown paper bag, all crunched up and shit. We figured that was the money for the past few days, because the man would just turn around and leave."

Teresa leans forward in her chair, resting her elbows on the table and gesturing her confusion with her hands. "Why didn't you just rob that man once he had the money?"

"Ohh yeah, we tried that. We started following that guy now. We followed him everywhere. Yesterday, we even followed him back to Hacienda Lane. He took a bunch of Chinese food into the house and came out like thirty minutes later. So we followed him to the other side of town, to a small storage place. We didn't see anybody else around, so we rolled up on him once he got out of his car. Tito got to him first and threw him on the ground, and we kicked the shit out of him. We looked all over for the money, but all he had was, like, seventy bucks in his wallet." He pauses, looking uncomfortable suddenly. After a moment, he continues, quieter now,

"Tito got real angry and started asking him where the money was. He said that he forgot to collect today. That he was in such a rush that he just forgot. Tito didn't believe him, and he started to slam the guy's head into the ground. He fucking killed him, man."

"Where's the man's body now?" asks Teresa. She has begun to chew on her bottom lip as her mind works through this new information.

"It's probably still there. Self Help Storage, in Katy. We opened his trunk and threw his body in. I didn't want to kill anybody, man. We were supposed to just beat the fucker up, and take the money. Tito got fucking crazy, though. He said that we should just go back to the house and roll up on the other two *vatos*. That they wouldn't expect us."

Teresa taps Gabriel on the shoulder and they confer with each other for a moment, then Teresa exits the room to call in the report of the dead body.

"Did you go back to the house?" asks Gabriel.

"Yeah, man. The van had already left, though. I went to peek in through a window and just saw some woman watching TV. She didn't look like no whore, though. We figured they went to the field already. Tito said that hitting them in the field was even better. That there would be no police around and shit!" The man laughs at the irony, but it quickly fades.

As Gabriel pushes back from the table slightly, fidgeting with the pen in his hand, he says, "Well, you were right. You took over two thousand dollars off the dead pimp, didn't you?"

"I didn't really have a chance to count it. We got hit by your guys before I knew what was happening. I honestly don't even remember shooting my gun," the man says in hushed tones as he stares at the table.

"We got the police going to check on the black Mercedes," says Teresa as she comes back in the room and sits down.

"He says he doesn't remember firing his gun," Gabriel tells her, pretending this information is surprising.

"Aww, honey," Teresa pins the man with a harsh glare, "that's because you didn't. While you were lying down in the front seat like a little bitch, it was your buddy Tito that shot Agent Bennett."

The prisoner sits up in his chair, a renewed excitement for life shining in his eyes. "That means that I won't do no life in prison?"

Just then, another agent enters the room and says that HPD already found the black Mercedes, with Luis' body found dead in the trunk.

Teresa turns on the prisoner again, her eyes like darts. "Aww, *papi*, you'll be going away for accessory to murder instead...three counts. Not quite life, but still a lot of years being someone's little bitch."

The man sinks back into his chair, realizing once again that he is going to prison.

CHAPTER TWELVE
ELENA'S HOUSE

Teresa peers through the passenger window at the white two-story house as she and Gabriel pull up at 116 Hacienda Lane. HPD patrolmen arrived first and secured the house while Teresa and Gabriel were finishing up the interrogation with their prisoner back at the office.

As they exit the car and walk toward the house, Gabriel comments, "Jesus, it looks just like any other house. I wonder if the neighbors even noticed seven women being shuttled back and forth every day."

"If they did, do you think they would have given a fuck?" retorts a downtrodden Teresa.

A patrolman near the front door informs them that there was only one person in the house when they first arrived on scene. "She says her name is Elena Flores, but she doesn't have any I.D."

Teresa sighs. "Alright. You find any signs that they were housing any other people here?"

"We found clothes inside, so far belonging to two different men. There's a shed out back, though...it looks like somebody's been living in it. It's pretty foul in there. There's a bucket of shit, and some ratty old blankets," replies the officer.

Uribe, who's just arrived on scene, walks up to the trio and taps Gabriel on the shoulder. "Hey, Gabe, let's talk for a minute."

Gabriel tenses, fearing the worst, but follows Uribe a few feet over to the front of the yard, to speak privately.

"Look, man, I'm gonna back you on the shooting. The guy was dead anyway; what's it matter that you put an extra one in his head? I'm gonna say that he was on his back, and it appeared that he was raising his weapon. At that point, you had no choice but to tap him again."

Gabriel deflates a little, visibly relieved.

Uribe isn't finished with him, though. "I just heard from headquarters. The District Office wants you to take a few days off. Just until the shooting board finishes its investigation."

Gabriel wants to argue but knows that it's out of Uribe's hands; he simply nods his head.

"Take a few days to relax, man. Go home, fuck your wife, have a few beers. You deserve it, man. That was a tremendous pull finding the field," says Uribe.

Wanting to change the subject, Gabriel asks, "Did somebody finally get ahold of Bennett's family?"

"Yeah, we had a couple agents from the local office up there in Dallas go over to his mom's house and tell her."

"How'd she take it?"

Uribe gives him a look. "How do you think? Flipped out...started crying. She's coming down tomorrow with Louis' sister to make the funeral arrangements."

Gabriel's shoulders slump; he still feels responsible. "Alright. Do me a favor and call me so I can meet up with them. I'll be off anyway, so I can help them with whatever they need."

"Yeah, sure, man. I'll call you when they're on their way to the morgue. Now get outta here. We're good, we got this," says Uribe, nodding toward the house.

Gabriel does as he is told. Uribe waits, watching as Gabriel gets in his car and drives away, before he catches up with Teresa. She is already inside the living room as Uribe enters the house.

"I don't know what you are talking about. This is my friend's house and I'm just crashing here for a few days," says the woman, Elena. She appears nervous, her eyes darting around as she speaks.

"Bullshit, sweetheart. Alger is *dead*. Rodrigo is back in a cell, and he gave you up. He told us all about how *you* and Luis are running these whores." As a scare tactic, Uribe holds up a photograph of Luis' dead body in the trunk of his car. "Luis is gone now, so it looks like you are gonna be the only one left holding the bag."

Elena's eyes grow wide and she draws in a ragged breath at the sight of Luis doubled over like a rag doll. Turning those large eyes on Teresa, she is adamant as she says, "No! That's a lie. I just feed the girls and clean them."

"So, what are you, then? A fucking caretaker?" shouts Teresa.

"*Si*. I take care of the girls. It was Rodrigo and Alger that would take them to the fields." Looking like a trapped animal, Elena's eyes flick between Teresa and Uribe. "Please, I used to be one of them. Believe me. I was so afraid, so I just did what they said."

Teresa crosses her arms over her chest, aiming for an intimidation pose. "Bullshit! You gotta give us more than a sob story, *chica*."

The woman gives an emphatic shake of her head. "I don't know anything."

"How do they get the girls in the country?" asks Uribe.

"I don't know. Honestly. A white guy shows up every once in a while with a new girl."

"Describe him. What kind of car does he drive?" asks Teresa as she removes a small notebook from her pocket.

"He's a white guy, I don't know. He's old. Like in his fifties. He has white hair and a large belly. He looks like any white guy." Elena shrugs apologetically, aware that she isn't giving them much to go on. "He would always drive up in a black SUV."

Uribe scoffs. "What, so he'd just bring the girls to the front door?"

"No. They would open the gate up for him and he'd drive around back. One time, I saw Alger go out there to help him take the girl out," Elena says, her eyes darting about nervously again.

Teresa lowers the notebook to peer at Elena. "What do you mean, help him take the girl out? Did they have her hidden in a box or crate or something?"

"No. He needed to take her out of the dash. Like she was under the dash, and they had to unscrew it to get her out and stuff," Elena says, using her hands to mime the removal of a makeshift lid.

"Jesus Christ! These girls are trapped in a fucking dashboard from Mexico to Houston?" Teresa blood is boiling, and she nearly snaps her pencil. With a renewed fire, she yells, "Come on, you need to give us more. What's the white man's name? You know more! What aren't you telling us?"

Flinching, Elena says, "I don't know his name. The girls called him Cucuy, but Alger would call him Jefe."

"The Boogeyman?" Teresa's jaw nearly hits the floor at the absurdity of the name.

Shooting Teresa a sideways glance, Uribe asks, "So, you would get the girls from Cucuy...then what?"

"They would take her out, then depending on what time she got here, they would either put her in the shed or take her straight to the field with the other girls."

A sudden thought strikes Uribe. "What happens when the girls get sick? What then?" he asks as he stares intently at the woman.

Elena looks down in shame, silent.

"What the hell would you do when they got sick?" Teresa shouts, nearly losing her cool.

As the woman cowers from Teresa's anger, her words come out in a rush. "Sometimes, the girls would get so sick that Rodrigo would just kill them. One time, a girl was in the shed and wouldn't stop coughing. It got so loud that Rodrigo was afraid she would wake the neighbors. He opened the gate and choked her to death."

"What did he do with the body?" yells Teresa.

"They rolled her up in some carpet and buried her with the others," Elena replies, her shoulders now shaking with heaving breaths as she breaks down in tears.

Faster than anyone can react, Teresa lunges at Elena with unbridled rage. As she straddles the helpless woman, she grabs Elena's throat with one hand and her hair with the other, twisting Elena's head until her neck almost breaks. Leaning in close, Teresa screams in her ear, "Where the hell did they bury their bodies?"

Flustered by the surprise attack, Uribe attempts to pull the small woman off of Elena, but even his much larger frame is no match for Teresa's fury. Only after an officer jumps in to help him are the two men able to subdue Hurricane Teresa.

Now completely terrified, Elena's voice is raw as she chokes out, "They buried them near the field where they would take the girls for sex. They would get one last day of work out of the girl and then make all the others dig a hole." She pauses as she has a coughing fit, her throat damaged from Teresa's iron grip. When it passes, she says, "They would put all the carpets in the hole and tell the girls that they would be getting new carpets. Then they would load the girls in the van except for the sick girl. Rodrigo would choke the girl until she died. He would cover the body with carpet and then bury her in the hole."

Agent Uribe is quick to react through the shock of the confession. Rodrigo has already been released to his bondsman, and two agents were assigned to tail him and see if he would lead them to his boss. Uribe whips his phone out tries to call them; Agent Norris answers. "Where the hell are you?" Uribe barks into the phone.

"We're sitting outside the Pie House on Kirby," replies Norris.

Uribe asks the agent, "You still have eyes on Rodrigo?"

"He went inside with the bondsman a few minutes ago. We can't see them from this angle."

Uribe's blood pressure skyrockets. Instinctively, he already knows it's too late, but into the phone he yells, "Get the fuck in there and arrest him, *now*! We've got a murder charge on him!"

Agents Norris and Wade are quick to exit their vehicle and rush into the restaurant. Around a corner and sitting at the counter is the bondsman. With their guns drawn, they demand to know where Rodrigo is.

Startled, the bondsman says that he is in the bathroom.

The two agents move toward the bathroom and kick the door in. As they tactically search and clear the bathroom, it becomes clear that he is nowhere to be found.

Little do they know, shortly after arriving, Rodrigo slipped out the back of the restaurant, where he had a cab waiting. Little does Rodrigo know, Gustavo and his partner are now following him; they have been with him since he was released. Aware that there was police surveillance on Rodrigo, the pair of assassins waited patiently for their opportunity.

Gustavo has orders to kill Rodrigo. Cartel upper management doesn't want any loose ends, and Rodrigo is just that; the cartel knows that it's just a matter of time before the feds build a stronger case against him. His ineptitude at protecting the girls from robbers didn't help his cause as the order was coming down.

Gustavo and his partner follow at a safe distance as Rodrigo directs the cab driver to an address off of the southwest freeway near the Galleria.

Uribe is furious as he gets word that Rodrigo slipped the tail. He notifies HPD and instructs them to put out an all-points bulletin for Rodrigo Washington. Then, cab companies are solicited for information as to any fares their cabbies may have had.

None of the fares for any of the city's cab companies match Rodrigo's description, but Uribe knows that doesn't mean much; a fifty-dollar bill and the threat of a cartel hit on his family would keep any cabby quiet.

Uribe takes custody of Elena, and has all police officers clear out of the house. "Alright, people, we have to get out of here, now. EVERYBODY OUT! If this fucker tries to come home, I want to nail his ass. Teresa, you post upstairs and make it seem like Elena is still here, up in her room. We'll have TAC teams two streets over, waiting for your signal. Rodrigo doesn't know that the shooter gave this place up. It might be a long shot, but he slipped his tail and might not have anywhere else to go."

The agents move into position and the HPD officers get in their cruisers and leave. In just a few moments, the house is just as it was before, except upstairs Teresa patiently waits to kill the man that she has grown to hate.

CHAPTER THIRTEEN
GABRIEL'S ANGEL

Gabriel stands at his bathroom sink as he brushes his teeth. The mirror is still fogged from the long, hot shower he just took. It was a much-needed respite from the awful day he just had.

He stares into the mirror with an almost catatonic gaze. He can't stop picturing Bennett's body, as he lay with blood slowly pouring from his neck. Trying to shake the image off, he finishes and rinses out his mouth. He removes the towel from around his waist and throws it over the shower curtain. After he puts on his deodorant, he gives himself a small spritz of cologne. As he walks into the bedroom, he takes care to not look over at Oolie, who's sitting up in bed with her back against the headboard. She pretends to be unfazed by his presence as she reads a book.

Trying to be casual, Gabriel attempts to seduce his wife. "Look, today was a pretty bad day. What I really want is some sex, and then to just pass out."

Immediately, her claws come out. "Is that the only reason you married me? To just come home and have sex with? Well, I didn't leave my country just to come here and fuck you whenever you want." She throws the book at him. "Why don't you just go out and fuck your little girlfriend, Teresa. I know you aren't always working when you say you are. There is no way that *the great Gabriel Granado* is always the one that has to go catch the criminals."

"Ohh, please—you're fucking crazy. You know what I do for a living, so don't give me that shit. Today we fucking killed two guys as they robbed a couple of pimps with a van full of fuckin' whores. While you sat here on your fat ass all day, I was out there in the hot sun, actually doing something." He scowls at the look of indignation that takes up her face. Tossing the book she threw back onto the bed, he angrily professes, "And don't give me shit about Teresa, I've never done anything with her. She's my fucking partner; I don't look at her like that."

Rapidly cycling through emotions, suddenly Oolie is tearful. "You're my husband...why don't you love me? You don't look at me anymore like you used to. You used to be so sweet. I thought I found the love of my life with you," she says, rising to her knees on top of the covers. She is attempting to reconcile with Gabriel, but he's beyond making amends at this point.

It's not sex with his wife that he wants tonight...it's sex with someone new. "No! Not after the day that I had, am I gonna put up with this shit. You wanna accuse me of fucking my partner? Well, go ahead. It just confirms how fucking psycho you've gotten. You wanna talk about changing? Look at you! All you do is sit around the house. Go the fuck out once in a while. I can't take this shit with you always being here," Gabriel sneers as he goes to the closet to put on jeans and a shirt.

Behind him, he can hear his wife begin to sob as she sinks back into the bed. When he announces that he's going out and will be back later...she just continues to cry. He doesn't react; the sight of his wife crying into her pillow isn't enough to distract him from what he really desires.

Before he leaves the room, he takes a moment to look at her one last time...and feels nothing. Once a man decides that he is going to go cheat on his wife, dopamine is released into his system. The only thing he wants after that is to keep that high for as long as possible. It's not even the act of sex that gets him going, it's setting it all in motion—that's the real juice.

After he puts on his shoes, he goes into the garage and opens the door of his truck. From behind the seat, he collects a small gym bag. Inside is what will round out his attire for the evening: A black baseball hat and a black hooded sweatshirt. Now prepped and ready, he gets in the driver's seat and heads for his favorite spot.

Most military men have a certain moral turpitude when it comes to paying women for sex, and Gabriel Granado is one of them. While in the military, he was not unlike other Navy men. He enjoyed his port calls in the Philippines, and Thailand—places where a man can receive a certain level of sexual fulfillment. His appetites were never really satisfied, though; he was never enchanted with the mystique of Asian women.

His career as an Immigration officer gives him a certain level of insight into what brothels are under investigation and which are not. The only one that has consistently passed his rigorous vetting process is "The Spa of Houston." As he drives toward the highway, he eagerly thinks about what tonight's line-up will be like. Are there any new girls? Are any of his regulars going to be there?

The thought of being caught and losing everything never really enters the forefront of his mind; it always lingers just on the outer limits, adding to the excitement of it all. It's not just the act of cheating that does it for Gabriel, it's the feeling of power, because after all, you don't pay a prostitute for sex—you pay them to leave afterwards.

Gabriel arrives at his destination. For fear of someone recognizing his truck in the spa's parking lot, he parks along the side of the used records store one building over. As he gets out of the truck, he carefully surveys the area; it's one a.m. and nothing good happens in Houston at one in the morning. He's on guard as he hastily walks to the spa's front entrance. As he opens the front door and steps inside, it automatically activates a doorbell chime. As he stands, waiting patiently at a large steel gate, he glances over at an ATM machine to his right. He snickers under his breath to himself about how many suckers actually use the machine, their bank information now being used by a third party in South America. The stolen information, along with the "tips" for the evening, result in one expensive piece of pussy for those men swindled by the machine.

When no models have appeared for the line-up after what feels like an eternity, he presses a small doorbell on the wall to his left and the chime rings again. This time, he hears a door at the far end of the building open as fluorescent light suddenly fills that part of the dark hallway behind the gate. He sees the silhouette of a petite woman walk toward him. She is alone and as she draws near, he can begin to make out her features. She is young and is wearing a small bikini. As is custom in this kind of place, the bikini is much too small; her areolas are partially exposed as she saunters to the gate. She stops and stands before him on the other side.

Her body illuminated by only a small black-light, he looks on in awe of her angelic form; this is a girl he's never seen before. Without saying a word, he removes three folded up twenty-dollar bills from his pocket and slides them through a slot in the gate. She reaches forward and collects the money, then presses a small button to her right and the gate buzzes open. As Gabriel enters the hallway, she turns around and leads him into a small room marked "3." With a cold, emotionless face, she looks at Gabriel and pats the massage table, and as he approaches it, she exits the room, closing the door behind her as she leaves.

He knows the process; this is when he is to get "comfortable." He starts by taking off his shoes and putting them under a small stool in the corner, then removes his keys and the other contents of his pockets and places them in his shoes for safekeeping. He unzips his sweater and carefully unclips his holster from his belt. Constantly keeping the holstered handgun concealed, he folds the sweater around it and gently lays the sweater on the stool.

He unbuckles his belt and unbuttons his jeans, then removes and carefully folds the jeans before placing them on top of the sweater. His shirt follows, and he lays it atop his jeans as well. Now standing almost completely naked, he debates removing his socks. He goes through this same song and dance every time he's here, and just like every other time, he looks at the dingy carpet and opts to leave his socks on.

Grabbing the folded-up towel at the foot of the massage table, he wraps it around his waist, starting to feel giddy. This is one of his favorite parts of the session: The wait before the model returns. The excitement is almost palpable, and he forces himself to sit on the edge of the padded table so that he doesn't pace back and forth.

He is beginning to feel that she is taking longer than usual to return, and much like a drug addict, his heart starts to beat faster. He attempts to calm himself by laying down on the massage table. As he stares at the mold-speckled ceiling tiles, he thinks, *Is tonight the night I get caught?*

Just then, the door opens, and he quickly rolls to lay on his side, facing the door. He is instantly relieved to see the woman as she comes in, small plastic shower caddy in hand. She closes the door and turns the small lock, ensuring that they won't be disturbed, then walks to a small table along the wall and sets the caddy down. She stands a few feet away, facing the table.

In this dim lighting, she is far enough that Gabriel can only just make out her face; she appears resigned to the fact that they are going to have sex, rather than enthusiastic. He normally likes a little bit of pageantry during his sessions but is excited nonetheless at the idea of ravaging this beautiful woman. Sensing that they are not really getting anywhere, he walks to his shoes and removes the two hundred dollars in twenties folded up inside. He places the money on the table next to the shower caddy and walks back to the massage table.

The woman picks up the money and begins counting it with care. She appears to be having trouble with her math, and starts over.

"It's two hundred, sweetheart," Gabriel murmurs. She looks at him for a moment, her eyebrows knit together, and resumes counting the money. Whispering to herself, she has begun to count aloud in Spanish as she places each bill, one by one, on the table, forming a small pile of money. As he watches, Gabriel asks, "Do you speak English?"

The girl looks at him with sad eyes and says, "No."

Continuing in Spanish, Gabriel says, "It's two hundred dollars."

Having ascertained a dollar amount, she now knows what he wants, and her hands develop a slight tremor as she carefully folds the money back up and places it under the shower caddy.

"What's your name?" Gabriel asks softly.

"Rosalie." She walks to Gabriel and stands face to face with him, then begins to remove her bikini top with one hand as she gently caresses his chest with the other.

Once her top is off, Gabriel stares at her breasts like a hungry man looking at a juicy steak. He asks her, "How long have you been working here?"

When she replies, "Since yesterday," a fresh wave of excitement washes over him; there's something tantalizing about helping to break in the new girls.

She gently pushes him to lay back on the table. As he leans back, he removes the towel from around his waist, revealing his engorged manhood. Now sprawled out on the table, he begins to massage her butt with his right hand as she stands beside him, watching while she removes a condom from the front of her bikini bottom and attempts to tear open the wrapper. Noticing she is having trouble, Gabriel gently takes the condom from her hands and carefully tears the packaging. He takes the wrapper and throws it on the floor as he hands the condom back to Rosalie.

She opens her mouth just enough to bite the tip and slowly bends over at the waist. As she attempts to unroll the condom down his shaft, she realizes too late that she has the condom facing the wrong direction. The unrolled condom is forced into the back of her mouth, gagging her. She straightens abruptly and spits the condom into her hands with a violent cough.

Losing interest in his hard on, Gabriel sits up on the table and glares at Rosalie, mystified that a whore could be so bad at basic things. He holds out his hand. "Give me the condom."

With her eyes watery from the coughing, she hesitatingly hands the condom over. He fidgets with it for a few moments, trying to find the correct end to roll from. He has become slightly limp from the break in action. "Get on your knees," he commands her.

It takes her several tries to do so, each time almost falling from losing balance in her high heels until she gets it right. When she is finally on her knees, Gabriel grabs her head in both hands and pulls it toward his unwrapped penis.

Suddenly developing a backbone, she puts out her hands and shoves backward off his thighs, yanking her head from his grasp. She glares at him, but remains kneeling before him. Gabriel knows what "no" means in a place like this, and refrains from grabbing her head again, like he wants to.

Slightly frustrated, he grabs her hand instead and places it on his penis, telling her to stroke it. She gives him a lackluster hand job, but it achieves its intended purpose regardless. Once more fully erect, he puts on the condom, then lays down on his back and tells her to get on top.

As she straddles him, he notices her wincing in pain as she slowly eases herself down on him, and he wonders how many men she must have been with today. She starts to thrust forward with slow, gentle movements, and repetitiously utter, "*Papi*"—not quite chanting it, but more saying it robotically.

Gabriel begins to regret his choice; he is losing interest in this lifeless engagement. Wanting to get his money's worth, he orders her off of him, and she quickly dismounts as he holds the condom on at the base of his shaft.

Thinking the session is over, Rosalie moves toward the shower caddy to clean herself. Behind her, Gabriel is on his feet almost as soon as she is. He grabs her by her hips, and in one fluid motion, picks her up and bends her over the massage table.

Frantically, she tries to push herself up, but his forearm is across her back. Her voice quivering with fear, she asks, "What are you doing?"

"We aren't done yet," he replies flatly.

She can feel him lining himself up with her back entrance. For a second, he raises his arm off her back and she thinks to reach for a panic button, but before she can, he grabs her waist again. His grip is so tight, it feels inescapable. Panic overwhelms her, ramping up in intensity at the raging fire in her backside as he spears himself into her. Her muscles contract involuntarily, and he moans at the same time she cries out, feeling as though she is tearing in half.

She is more terrified than she ever was in the field; at least in the field, she had the men protecting her, if only in their own interests. At least in the field, she had the other women, their shared pain somewhat comforting. In this room, she is alone. The cold air and soft couch to sleep on seem insignificant now; in this moment, she can't help but wish she was back home with her mother, far away from this terrible place.

Without tenderness, Gabriel continues to impale the small girl. Her knees have buckled, her body in shock, and he and the massage table are all that hold her up. She has no fight left in her, and she resigns herself to the fact that she is nothing more than a series of holes to please random men. She stares straight ahead at the mirrored wall in front of her, where her own face stares back. She looks like a wild animal, desperate and damaged. It is too painful to look at herself, but she can also see Gabriel behind her; she watches him instead. His eyes are closed as he continues to ram himself deeper and deeper into her. She closes her eyes, too, and tries not to focus on the incredible pain that knocks the breath out of her with each stabbing thrust. A detached sort of numbness overcomes her, and she welcomes it.

A few minutes later, in the darkness behind her eyes, she hears him grunt loudly as though from far away as he thrusts deep into her one last time and begins to spasm. She opens her eyes and looks at Gabriel as he stands still, enjoying his bit of tranquility. After a few short moments, he begins to pull away from her.

"Fuck! The condom broke," Gabriel spews in English. He quickly moves to the shower caddy and rips off a paper towel to remove the broken condom from his penis, then begins to furiously spray his entire groin with the rubbing alcohol. He rashly grabs a few baby wipes, and in his haste drops the package on the floor. He uses the wipes that he removed to clean himself, and then repeats the whole process by spraying more alcohol on his crotch.

Rosalie bends over to pick up the package of baby wipes, and sucks in a sharp breath as she feels the intense sting once again in her backside. She is sure that she won't be able to handle the alcohol in Zoe's normal cleaning ritual; a cold shower would be more appropriate.

As Gabriel feverishly cleans himself, she removes a baby wipe. Ever bashful, she turns away and begins to clean herself gingerly, careful not to wipe too hard where her skin has broken.

Once he is satisfied that he won't be bringing a disease back to his wife, Gabriel begins to put on his clothes. Careful to not expose his gun, he turns away while she puts on her bikini top and quickly finishes dressing. He stands by the door, watching while Rosalie attempts to put on her bikini bottom.

She leans against the wall while navigating her foot through one of the leg holes. Standing there looking like a flamingo, she keeps getting her high heel caught in the fabric. Gabriel can't help but laugh at the sight of her fumbling around, but it's cut short when he notices her distressed expression and the odd, tense way she holds herself. Before losing her balance, she finally gets her legs through both holes and pulls the bikini up to her waist.

Avoiding his eyes, she walks to the door and unlocks it, but before she can open it, Gabriel stops her. He cups each side of her face with his hands and says in Spanish, "Sorry if I was rough."

Rosalie looks at him with a raw, uncompromising stare, and remains quiet. For a moment, he forgot there's no romance in a place like this. Remembering the social compact of a whore house, he realizes that he's worn out his welcome. He releases her face and adjusts his clothes one last time as she opens the door. They both exit the room into the hallway.

CHAPTER FOURTEEN
CROSSFIRE

Rodrigo stretches out in the back seat of the cab and takes a few minutes to rest his eyes, completely unaware that Gustavo and his partner are following close behind.

Gustavo orders his partner to back away and give the cab some room. On Highway 59, traveling toward the south side of Houston, he realizes there's only one place Rodrigo could be headed. Gustavo takes out his cell phone and dials a number. The other end rings a few times, then an answer. He says, "Hector, look, *mano*, we found Rodrigo. That little *puto* is headed to you."

"What do you want me to do? Let him in?" asks Hector.

"*Si*. When he comes to the door, you let him in like nothing's wrong. Act like you don't know shit about the police. You got any customers in right now?"

"Yeah, there are three johns in sessions and one girl in the break room."

Gustavo rubs his chin as he thinks this over. "OK. You gotta play it cool. Don't let him get spooked. Take him to your office."

"How long do you need me to keep him here?" asks Hector.

"Hector..." Gustavo pauses, then sighs. "You're gonna have to step up and take care of him."

Uneasy, as Gustavo expected, Hector is quick to avoid the request. "What do you mean? How long till you get here? I can keep him here till you show up."

"Look, *mano*, don't be a *pinche maricon*. We can't come in there and blast him, cuz you got customers. He'll see us rollin' up on the monitors, so you gotta do it. Now *man* the fuck up. He's pulling into the back lot now. Call us when it's done."

———

Watching the surveillance monitors, Hector sees the cab pull up. He closes his eyes, breathing in deeply through his nose, and summons the courage and the rage he locked away long ago. Into the phone, he says, "I got it," and hangs up.

Hector thought his days of killing were over. He did his time in the trenches as a soldier; now, he spends his days running whores. On bad days, he has to deal with a toilet overflowing from used tampons, or a John that got too rough on a girl without paying for it. Now, he's expected to kill a man.

He stands up from his small rolling chair and looks around the office for a suitable weapon. He doesn't keep a gun in the place, on the off chance that there's a police raid, and a letter opener will be too messy. He thinks about doing it old school...using his hands to strangle Rodrigo. Remembering that Rodrigo is half his age, and in good shape, that idea fizzles out quick.

Answering the door with his "Bitch Stick" will be too suspicious. The small billy-club standing in the corner of his office got the moniker "Bitch Stick" from the very whores it has protected. Hector has been forced to use it on more than one occasion when a client wants a refund, or gets too rough with a girl, and it just so happens that black men have always been the recipients of its wrath.

He hears the back bell ring and looks over to the surveillance monitors. The monitor switches to show the back camera, and Hector can see Rodrigo waiting as he scans the dark parking lot for danger. He notices that Rodrigo is wearing a sling from the gunshot wound to his shoulder, and it gives him an idea.

He heads to the break room, where Juicy lays asleep on the couch, and opens the drawer of bikinis. Hector's confidence now swims in a sea of boldness as he casually removes a bikini bottom from the drawer, then walks to the back entrance. Hector has killed twelve men in his lifetime. The only mercy they got was death itself; with a strong body, and the intemperance found only in youth, he was a brutal killer. However, that was the past. After he became manager of the spa, he lost the fire that made him famous within the cartel. He became a pimp, and a pimp is only a god over whores and johns. His influence extends to an area of two thousand square feet, no more. He's been a shell of his former self.

As he approaches the back door, he gets himself back to center. Now completely focused, he opens the door and casually throws the bikini bottom across his right shoulder. "Rodrigo! Two days in a row? Maybe it was that hug I gave you, no?"

"Look, *mano*, I need to come inside." Rodrigo is curt in response, his eyes shifting nervously.

As he turns to his side and motions for Rodrigo to come inside, Hector says, "You can come anywhere you want, *guapo*."

Rodrigo is instantly disarmed by Hector's flirtation. It's widespread knowledge that Hector is gay, and he has flirted with Rodrigo before. He steps inside and heads straight for Hector's office, paying no attention as Hector rigs the back door to stay ajar.

When Hector makes it back to his office a moment later, Rodrigo is already sitting in the rolling chair, closely watching the suite of surveillance monitors. They show nothing but three johns at various stages of fuck. When Hector enters the room, Rodrigo spins around in the chair to face him. "Lock the door," Rodrigo barks.

Under any other circumstances, Hector would have put Rodrigo in his place for ordering him around, but instead he turns to close the door and rotates the lock. As he turns back to Rodrigo, his voice coming out sultry, he says, "No one will bother us now."

As he intended, Hector struck a nerve with the man, and Rodrigo spins the chair back around to face the monitors as he tries to hide his disgust.

Hector slowly approaches Rodrigo from the rear. "So, what happened to your shoulder? You want me to take a look at it for you?"

"Some fucking *pendejos* robbed us at the spot. They killed Alger."

Making sure to sound surprised, Hector asks, "What does Luis say to do?"

"I can't get ahold of him. I just called the number for the attorney and he got me bailed out. They only have a bullshit weapons charge on me," Rodrigo says, his eyes still focused on the monitors.

"And you came here, you stupid *puto*? The police probably followed you here!" Hector says as he smacks the back of Rodrigo's head. Still playing like this is news to him, he leans forward to watch the monitors, as though searching for cops.

"No, *mano*. The police *were* following me. I lost them and came here," says Rodrigo, defensive and more than a little offended at being treated like an idiot.

"Look, man, we can't be fucking around with no police. You need to get the fuck outta here."

"I know, alright? I just need some money and your car to get close to the border. When I finally get ahold of Luis, he can get me back into Mexico," Rodrigo pleads, turning toward Hector.

Glancing at the monitor behind Rodrigo, Hector feigns shock and points. "Fucking police!"

Lightning-fast, Rodrigo spins the chair back around, but sees nothing on the monitors. Standing just behind Rodrigo, Hector is too far away from his club. Thinking fast before Rodrigo turns back to him, he snatches up a small snow-globe from the shelf to his right and smashes it across the back of Rodrigo's head. Stunned, Rodrigo attempts to stand, but Hector is quick—he throws Rodrigo face-first on the floor, before the man can regain his sharpness.

Hector jumps on Rodrigo's back and straddles him, bikini bottom clenched in his fist. He swaddles Rodrigo's neck with the bikini bottom and pulls back as hard as he can. Blood is smeared on the back of his hand, and he realizes he must have cut it on the snowglobe when it broke, but he ignores it and pulls harder.

Rodrigo tries to fight him for several minutes, and Hector struggles to keep his hold against the man's bucking body, but finally, Rodrigo goes limp. Only after he is sure Rodrigo isn't playing possum, his cheek pressed to the floor and his eyes staring ahead lifelessly, does Hector loosen his grip on the fabric.

Adrenaline still courses through his veins as he looks down at his bloody hand. He feels no pain now but can sense the throbs as blood pours out. He wraps his weapon around the wound, using it as a bandage. Slightly lightheaded as he stands, he pulls his phone from his pocket and calls Gustavo. "It's done," he says, and hangs up just as quickly, then tosses the phone on his desk.

Hector plops down into his chair, his chest rising and falling heavily, and enjoys the momentary rapture that comes right after a kill. Soon, he knows, the neurotic terror of getting caught will consume his every thought.

Gustavo and his partner pull into the parking lot and back up to the rear entrance. Exiting the passenger side, he tells his partner to stay and keep the car running. As he walks by the back of the car, he knocks on the trunk. His partner releases the trunk lock and it pops open.

Gustavo enters the spa from the rear entrance and carefully surveys the area. Removing his gun from its holster, he slowly opens the office door. Rodrigo's lifeless body lays sprawled on the floor, and Hector is sitting in the chair, looking like a man who just climbed a mountain, equal parts fatigue and euphoria.

Stepping into the room, Gustavo says, "Nice work, *mano*. The old Hector never left, huh?"

"It's been five years since I killed someone. Too bad it had to be this pretty motherfucker. I'd have liked to turn him into a good little bottom." Hector sighs, rubbing Rodrigo's butt with his foot.

Gustavo scowls. "OK, man. Enough of that gay shit. Let's get him out to the trunk. Grab his feet."

Hector stands and unwraps the bikini from around his hand to check the wound.

"Ahh, *mano*, you got cut pretty good there. We'll take care of this *puto*, and get it stitched up. I'll call the vet to come by and look at you after we leave."

Hector nods and takes up position at Rodrigo's feet, bending to grab him by the ankles. Gustavo at the head, gripping Rodrigo's sling, they lift Rodrigo's body and maneuver it into the hallway. Before Gustavo can back out of the rear entrance, the sling works its way loose and Rodrigo's whole upper body smacks hard against the floor.

Just as Gustavo is trying to get a grip under Rodrigo's armpits, Gabriel exits his modeling room. As he glances toward the back of the hallway, the two villains freeze, paralyzed momentarily with shock. Immediately, Gabriel reaches for his gun, shouting at them to stop. Gustavo reacts before Hector, and goes for his own gun.

Gabriel is slightly faster and draws down on the two men. "I said stop!"

Gustavo ignores this second command, swiftly removing his gun from its holster, and attempts to aim at Gabriel. Without hesitation, Gabriel fires two rounds into Gustavo, hitting his chest and stomach.

As the shots fire, Hector dives sideways into his office and grabs his club. Bringing a club to a gun fight isn't the wisest idea, but he's out of options.

"Get the fuck out here!" Gabriel screams down the hallway. A door to his left opens and an old man in room two exits, hands raised in the air. "No! Damn it, get the hell back in your room," Gabriel orders. The old man obliges.

Gustavo's partner rushes in through the back entrance while Gabriel is distracted by the old man. The hitman fires three rounds at Gabriel, but misses high.

"Fuck!" Gabriel flinches at the unexpected gunfire but recovers quickly, unloading six rounds at the would-be assassin, striking him twice in the chest and once in the neck. The man falls to the ground, already dead. Realizing that he needs to seize the moment—with every second that passes, the man in the back office prepares his defenses—Gabriel quickly moves through the dimly lit hallway and takes note of the two men lying on the ground outside the office door, near the first dead body. They both appear to be no threat. Instead, he focuses his attention on the heavy breathing in the office. "Alright, motherfucker, put down your weapon and come out," orders Gabriel.

There is no response, but the heavy breathing has stopped. Gabriel peeks his head around the door frame—he sees nothing but an empty office. He pivots his whole body so that it's just outside the doorway. With his gun raised, he enters the room. From his left, a club swings toward his head. Managing to duck, he evades the blow but loses his balance and falls backwards onto the dead bodies.

Hector moves in for the death blow and raises the club above his head. Faster than Hector is, Gabriel raises his gun and fires four rounds into Hector's torso, just as the club-wielding man drives his body weight down upon Gabriel. Hector lands squarely on top of Gabriel, his final breath wheezing out of him. Sandwiched between death, Gabriel takes a brief moment to compose himself, but too late—a loud crack resounds in the dingy hallway, and so ends his life.

Gustavo manages to pull his legs out from under the dead federal agent. Coughing up blood bubbles, he knows that it's all over for him; none of his options are promising. He can get in the car and drive away, only to pass out behind the wheel. The police would probably patch him back up, but then he would stand trial for murdering a cop. That's no kind of life to live.

Sitting up against the wall at the back of the hallway, he raises his gun to his open mouth. For the briefest of moments, he thinks he sees an angel, just before he pulls the trigger.

Rosalie stands in the doorway of the modeling room she shared with Gabriel, staring at the blood that splatters the wall behind Gustavo's head.

CHAPTER FIFTEEN
FALLOUT

Minutes after Gustavo takes his own life, HPD patrolmen are first on scene; the client in room one decided to cut his losses and call the police. Better to risk arrest on a solicitation charge than die in a shootout.

The four prostitutes and three johns are rounded up and held in the backs of squad cars while police try to make sense of the crime scene. Not long after, Agent Uribe arrives, completely dismayed by the news of Gabriel's death. A patrolman lifts up the yellow police tape for him and points to the front entrance. "Detective Barahona is inside," he says.

Uribe manages a solemn nod, then walks inside. Crime scene investigators have set up flood lights, harshly illuminating the hallway. Uribe grimaces at the thought that this is where one of his agents met his end. As he walks past the open steel gate, he can see a crime scene technician photographing the pile of dead bodies at the other end of the hall. There lies Gabriel, still sandwiched between Hector and the bodies of Rodrigo and an unknown man; Gustavo sits upright in the nearby corner, glassy eyes staring at nothing.

Detective Barahona exits the office and steps over the mess of bodies, toward Uribe. "You must be Agent Uribe."

Uribe nods.

"Sorry about your man. It's a fuckin shame," he says.

Uribe quietly accepts his condolences as he surveys the hallway. "What do you know so far?" he asks.

Barahona shrugs. "We didn't get much from the whores or johns, because they didn't see shit. They all pretty much said the same thing: Shots popped off, and they heard a man yell down the hallway, then more shots. Come on back here, I'll show you the surveillance video."

As the two men navigate the dead bodies and enter the office, Barahona adds, "We couldn't figure out why your man was here without backup. We assumed he was doing some kind of undercover sort of thing, but then we watched the tapes. You see, each room has a camera hidden above the door, facing toward the massage table. They record everything. I bet these guys would stay the fuck away if they knew that."

As Barahona tells the computer technician seated at the desk to pull up the footage from room three, Uribe's stomach sinks. Still, a part of him refuses to believe what he already knows.

"Once, we saw this, we realized why he was here."

As the video plays back footage of Gabriel having sex with the small whore, confirming his fear, Uribe can't deny the truth and his shame burns hot.

The technician forwards the video to the end of the session, just before Gabriel exits the room, and pauses it. "This is where your man comes out of the room and sees the two perps moving the body," Barahona tells him.

The technician cues up footage of the hallway. The vantage point is from the front of the hallway facing the rear door. In the foreground is Gabriel, and in the distance, Hector and Gustavo can be seen moving Rodrigo's body.

"Looks like the taller one killed old boy in the office, and they were in the process of moving the body. They had a car outside with a third perp waiting in the driver's seat, and the trunk open. They had a bit of unfortunate luck right here; they dropped the body. As you can see, it's just as your man is coming out of his room. There's no audio, but the john that called 9-1-1 said he heard someone shout STOP really loud just before the first shots."

Uribe stares transfixed at the replay of Gabriel's last minutes alive, right up until the moment Gustavo points his gun at Gabriel's head. Uribe tears his eyes away; only from his peripheral view can he see the flash of the gunshot cross the screen. After a few moments, he looks back and watches the tail end of the encounter. There is the slightest satisfaction in watching Gustavo take his own life, but it pales in comparison to the loss he feels. As the clip ends, he turns back to Barahona. "What now?"

"It's a pretty open and shut case, in my opinion. It looks like a simple cartel hit, gone wrong. Both these guys are definitely enforcers, and the other mope just runs the whore house. We haven't I.D.'d the fourth guy yet."

"He's Rodrigo Washington. We were trying to pick him back up on some possible murders out near a field he was whoring women at."

Barahona nods, the pieces fitting together. "Well, there you go. He got clipped for being a fuck up. Your man just picked a bad night to get his dick wet."

Uribe is faced with an unfortunate situation. Once the press gets all the facts, Gabe's reputation will be tarnished. Not to mention, the integrity of Immigration agents as a whole. This won't simply be a black eye; heads will be on the chopping block. "Who all has seen these tapes?" he asks Barahona.

"Well, just the three of us." Barahona points at the computer technician.

"Look, man. He's got a wife. How's she gonna feel, knowing that her husband got gunned down just after he got done fucking a whore? I mean, come on, he was just in here to get a piece of ass. We need to focus on the good shit. He took down *three* cartel members, after they committed a murder," Uribe pleads.

The technician remains quiet, but Barahona looks uneasy. "I don't know. I mean, I don't want to disgrace the guy, but I can't really cover anything up."

Uribe tries again, appealing to the commonality of mistakes in human nature. "Come on, man. You've never cheated on your wife? You've never done something that you wish you could take back? Gabe paid the price already. It's not gonna do anybody any good to paint him in a light other than that of a hero. He is a fucking hero. He took down bad guys, doing bad things. None of us are goddamn angels. He fucked up, but he did real good."

"What are we supposed to do? Just erase the tapes?" asks Barahona, gesturing at the monitors and looking at Uribe like he must be nuts.

"Not all of them, of course not," Uribe backtracks, shaking his head. "Just get rid of the tape of him banging the whore, and I'll go break the camera in the fuck room. It'll look like he was just doing some reconnaissance of the brothel. I'll say that I sent him here to see if any of the girls knew anything about the sex field."

The men look at each other as they contemplate Uribe's plan. Dirtying up a crime scene isn't unheard of, but it's a delicate matter, and things can get out of hand rather quickly. "What about the girl he fucked? Won't she contradict your story?" Barahona counters.

"Let me worry about that."

The standoff continues, each man hoping the other will make the decision. Finally, Barahona relents. "OK. Him fucking the whore doesn't add any value to the case." As though trying to convince himself that this is the right course of action, he says, "It had nothing to do with the murder. We don't need any video of him in the room with the girl."

On Barahona's order, the technician takes measures to remove the recording in question as Barahona and Uribe walk silently to room three. Uribe reaches up to the pinhole camera as Barahona stands guard in the doorway, and a simple snip of a wire with his pocket knife does the trick. The camera being disabled can be explained away by something as simple as a random john discovering it, and in not wanting to be recorded, cutting the wire. "There, that should do it."

Barahona looks uneasy again.

Uribe sighs. "Look, man. We are doing the right thing here. We can't let him go down like that. It's a fucking disgrace."

Barahona nods, but with discouragement, and they return to the small office to check the status of the purge. The computer technician simply gives them a thumbs up when they comes through the door.

"What do we know about the whore he was with?" Uribe asks, wanting to get the other loose end taken care of.

Barahona shakes his head. "Nothing. She's been quiet since we arrived."

"You mind if we go have a chat with her?"

"No, by all means," says Barahona. He leads Uribe out to the squad car that Rosalie is sitting in.

Uribe opens the door and rests his forearm along the top of it as he leans down to speak with her. "What's your name?" he asks in English.

She remains silent, staring at the headrest of the seat in front of her.

"Look, the silent treatment won't help you. You're not in trouble. We just wanna find out what happened here," Uribe tries.

Rosalie continues staring ahead, her mouth shut.

Uribe becomes frustrated but remains calm. Closing the door on her, he walks away to regroup.

"I told ya, she isn't talking," says Barahona.

"Let's see if we can get somewhere with one of the other girls," Uribe grumbles, already walking off. Barahona follows him to another squad car nearby, and Uribe opens one of the back doors.

Inside, Zoe has been sitting for over an hour. Still rattled from the night's events, she nervously fidgets with a string from her bikini top.

"What's your name?" asks Uribe.

She perks up, hoping she'll be let out of the car. "Zoe."

"Well, Zoe, can you tell us about what happened?"

Zoe sighs heavily and slouches back down in her seat. "It's like I told the other cop, I was in a session when the gun went off. I didn't see anything."

"Yeah, we saw the surveillance video. We know you were in mid-fuck with that old guy, so we don't really care about you. We know that girl over there saw something, but she isn't talking. I can't help her if she doesn't cooperate," Uribe tells her, pointing toward Rosalie across the way.

Seeing he means Rosalie, she says, "She's a new girl they brought over from Mexico. She's scared because she thinks her family will get killed if she talks."

"Does she speak English?"

"No, she's literally fresh over the border. Yesterday was her first day."

"Alright, sit tight. We'll be back in a bit," says Uribe, tapping his knuckles on the roof of the car as he mulls over what she said. Standing, he shuts the door and turns to Barahona. "What do you think, Detective?"

Barahona rubs his chin, looking up at the stars while he considers. "Well, we know why they murdered Washington. She isn't gonna give us any more in that department. She's more valuable to you federal guys if she knows anything about their network, although she probably don't know shit. She doesn't look like she's on drugs…she probably got snatched up on the other side, sent here to get turned out."

"Yeah, but she's still part of your investigation. I'd like to have one of my female agents take a run at her, and see what she has on the smuggling."

"Be my guest. You're gonna have to coach her on what to say about Granado anyway. As far as I'm concerned, you can take custody of her. I want to get as far away from what we just did as possible," Barahona says, physically taking a step back from Uribe.

Already turning back toward Rosalie's squad car, Uribe tells him, "Don't worry about that. It's not gonna come back on you guys."

They say a man dies two deaths. One when his physical body ceases to live, the other when the last person to remember him dies. Gabriel Granado will be remembered as a hero to many, but to a few he will be truly seen, flaws and all. For Rosalie, he will be remembered as one of the many devils in her life. In protecting Gabriel's honor, Uribe has unwittingly been yet another champion of misery for Rosalie. A long life ahead for someone so young, a dark road for someone so pure, Rosalie's innocence was not taken with her virginity; it was taken when good men failed to be good men.

CHAPTER SIXTEEN
FALSE SALVATION

Alone in his office, the events of the last twelve hours finally catch up to Uribe as he leans back in his chair. His forearm lays across his closed eyes as he replays the clip of Gabriel dying in his mind. The flash from the gun leaves a spot that dances around as he tries to look away from the memory. A knock at the door jars him from his moment of solitude. It's Teresa; she's returned from the house on Hacienda Lane.

"Come in," he says.

Teresa enters. She closes the door and sits in a small chair to the right of his desk. "So, what the hell happened? Why did you send Gabe in there alone?"

"There's some stuff that's gonna fuck with you. You can't let it." He pierces her with a hard stare, trying to gauge if she'll be able to handle this or not.

She leans forward in frustration. "Uribe, what the fuck? Spit it out."

"I didn't send Gabe there."

Confused, she asks the obvious question: "Well, then what was he doing?"

Uribe closes his eyes and slumps against his chair, then looks up at the ceiling. He didn't want to have to spell it out for her, but it looks like he may have to. "Come on, Teresa. You know what he was doing there."

"No! What?" She stands abruptly, disgusted that he would suggest such a thing about her friend. "He wasn't like that. He has a wife, for Christ's sake!"

"They all have wives. It doesn't change the fact that he was a good man," Uribe sighs, suddenly feeling the exhaustion of the whole situation taking hold.

She begins to pace back and forth in disbelief. "No. I don't buy it. It must be a mistake. He was probably there looking for something to go on."

"Teresa, there was a surveillance camera recording him with the whore. The video showed him paying her for sex, and everything else. It was Gabe...plain as day."

Speechless and looking stricken, Teresa collapses into the chair again.

She looks as defeated as Uribe feels. Hoping to ease it for her, he says, "I talked the detective and one of the crime scene techs into erasing the tape. They realized that it didn't help or hurt their investigation."

It has the opposite effect. She stares at him, mouth agape, like he's sprouted a second head. "Why the hell did you do that?"

He scoffs. "Because, I'm not gonna let one bad thing define him. He fucked up and did some dirt. We all have. Who the fuck are we to judge him? He's our brother, and I'm not gonna have his entire life reduced to a fucking punchline."

Teresa slumps back in the chair. She doesn't like it, but she doesn't argue.

"I would do the same for you, and so would he. Now you take a few minutes to get yourself right with this," Uribe says as he stands and goes to the door to give her some privacy. Before he opens the door to leave, he looks back and says, "The whore he was with is in room two. She doesn't speak any English. When you're ready, go in and talk to her. See what she knows about the smuggling. When you're done, we'll send her down for processing."

After he exits the room and closes the door, Teresa closes her eyes, exhaling deeply. She wonders what other lies she is going to have to cover up.

When she gets herself correct, she walks out the door and heads for interrogation room two.

Rosalie sits on a cold metal chair. Still wearing a bikini, her body shivers as the exposed parts of her butt press against the seat. A small wool blanket is draped across her shoulders. She sits staring at her reflection in the two-way mirror. During their downtime, Zoe applied mascara on Rosalie's eye lashes. The sweat from sex and her tears have caused the make-up to streak down her face. She tries to wipe away the tracks of her tears, but only makes it worse, smearing her cheeks with darkness. All she can do is sit and look at the woman she has become, too soon.

When Teresa enters the room, she stands in silence for a moment and stares at Rosalie; she is astonished at how young the girl looks. Remembering why she's there, Teresa sits down across from her and sets down a small pad of paper. In Spanish, she asks, "What's your name, honey?"

Rosalie remains quiet.

"I'm a police officer. I'm not going to hurt you. What's your name?"

She drops her eyes to the table and whispers, "Rosalie Bolanos."

"OK, Rosalie. Where are you from?"

"Cochoapa El Grande."

"How long have you been working at the spa?"

Rosalie shifts in her seat, obviously uncomfortable at the mention of the spa. "Since yesterday."

Noting this, Teresa asks, "How old are you?"

"Sixteen."

Shocked by the answer, Teresa stops writing on her pad for a moment and stares at Rosalie again. A million thoughts fly through her head at once, not least of which that Gabriel might have deserved what he'd gotten in the end. Collecting herself, she asks, "Did you cross the border on your own?"

Remembering her father's face, Rosalie's eyes begin to well up. "No," she whimpers.

Teresa stands and brings her chair around to sit alongside Rosalie. Taking the young girl's hand from her lap, she holds it with both of hers. "You are safe now. I'm not gonna let anybody hurt you."

Rosalie wants to believe her, more than anything in the world, but her heart aches more and more with every broken promise of safety. Doubtful that Teresa is any different, she pulls her hand free from Teresa's embrace. She pulls the blanket tighter around herself and looks back to her reflection.

Teresa watches Rosalie's face, dazed by the obvious pain the young girl is feeling. "I'm not going to let you down. I promise, you are safe now," she swears.

Rosalie just sits, silently judging the situation.

Reaching for the pad of paper again, Teresa asks, "Where's your family?"

Rosalie can't hold back the tears any longer; they stream down her face like a waterfall. Aside from the tears, she remains stoic; she doesn't sob or whimper at all. She simply continues to stare at her own wet, shiny face in the mirror.

"Did they kill your family when they took you?" asks Teresa.

Rosalie's voice is shaky as she whispers, "My father."

Teresa looks up at her own reflection in the mirror. She knows that she will never fully be able to comprehend the pain Rosalie has felt. She can't simply hug Rosalie and take away all of her sadness; it's not that simple. She continues with the questioning, instead. "Tell me how it happened."

Rosalie sniffles, sitting up straighter, and says, "It doesn't matter now. He's already dead."

Teresa looks to the mirror again, hoping for a knock. Hoping that someone will be able to guide her through this awful journey.

There is no knock. There is nothing but a devastated girl, and a sad tale. "Tell me what happened, and I promise I'll never let them touch you again."

Rosalie turns her head and stares into Teresa's brown eyes; they remind her of her mother's. Rosalie's lips begin to quiver from holding back her story. At last, she relents. "Men came to our home, and killed my father. They said they would do terrible things to my mother if I didn't go with them."

"When was this?" asks Teresa, watching her intently.

"A week ago. They put me in a truck and took me to a man called Rey."

"Did they rape you?"

"No. My mother told me to act sick, so they wouldn't have sex with me. Rey took me and another girl, and put us in his car. We drove for hours. The whole while, Rey kept looking at me in the mirror. I kept coughing and he would yell at me to stop. After it got dark, we stopped at a small hotel and he put us in a bed together. He sat in a chair in the corner of the dark room and stared at us as we tried to sleep." She pauses, fidgeting with the edge of the blanket, and a tear falls into her lap. When she speaks again, her voice is barely audible. "After Celeste fell asleep, he stood up and sat next to me on the bed. I couldn't move. I wanted to cough, but he whispered for me to be quiet. He put his lips close to mine and slid his hand down the front of my pants. All I could smell were the cigarettes on his breath as he drooled on me and told me to spread my legs. He began to touch me down there and I begged him to stop."

"Did he stop?" asks Teresa, staring wide-eyed at Rosalie, her hand hovering just above the forgotten pad of paper.

"Only once I started to pee on his hand. He screamed at me and called me a dirty little bitch. He took his hand out of my pants and shoved his fingers in my mouth. I started crying and he picked me up and threw me into the bathroom. He told me to sleep in the tub."

"Did he hurt Celeste?"

Rosalie looks down in shame, as if she could have helped Celeste but chose not to. "I heard them through the wall. She begged him to stop and cried really loud. He must have put a pillow over her head because her voice got much quieter, until all I could hear was him moaning." She pauses again, almost angrily wiping at the tears on her face. "He didn't come to get me until the morning. He put us in the car and yelled at her every time she started crying."

"Was it Rey that took you over the border?"

Rosalie stares silently at her own reflection again, until Teresa repeats the question and it jars her out of her moment of silence. "No. Rey gave us to another man. A man named Cucuy."

Teresa quickly flips through her notes. "Is he a white man with gray hair?"

"Yes," replies Rosalie, new tears running down her face.

Sensing this is an open wound, Teresa haltingly asks, "What happened with Cucuy?"

The child's voice quivers. "Rey gave us to him and drove away. He seemed so nice as he took us in the building with the beds. He kept smiling and telling us what was going to happen, but then he took Celeste and tied her to a pole. He said he couldn't take her to America today."

She knows Rosalie is skirting something she doesn't want to say. She helps her along, asking, "He took you instead?"

"Yes...he took me," Rosalie whispers; the words hold a gravity that doesn't belong in them.

"Did he hurt you?" asks Teresa.

Rosalie wipes roughly at her eyes again, trying desperately to wipe the barrage of memories from her mind. "As much as they all did."

"How did he get you across the border?"

"He put me in the front of the truck. Inside the top part."

There's a sudden knock on the mirror, from the other side. "I'll be right back," Teresa tells Rosalie as she walks to the door and exits the room.

Outside, Uribe holds a laptop computer. "I've got this cued up to the driver's license photos of every man with a black SUV who's crossed the border in the past two weeks and fits the description of Cucuy."

"Let's hope they aren't getting across with fake IDs." Teresa takes the laptop and reenters the interrogation room. Sitting down next to Rosalie again, she opens the computer and sets it down in front of the girl. "Rosalie, I'm going to show you some pictures. Tell me if one of these men is Cucuy."

Rosalie looks on as the screen scrolls, half hoping to find her monster, half hoping to never see his face again. After a few moments of scrolling, he appears. She points. "That's him. That's Cucuy."

Teresa takes the computer and clicks on the picture. "Jeffrey Floding of Laredo. You are sure that this is him?" Looking over at the young girl, fresh tears welling up in her eyes, Teresa gets the only answer she needs. She puts her arms around the broken child and pulls her close.

Rosalie lets loose and cries into Teresa's chest as if she is her mother. All Teresa can do is caress the tormented young girl's back and wait for the tears to subside; she has earned her sadness and needs to let it out. She needs to make room for a lifetime of sorrow.

Uribe enters the room and looks at the computer screen. "That's Cucuy?"

At the sound of his voice, Rosalie flinches. Teresa shushes her, cradling Rosalie's head against her bosom as the girl begins to cry harder, and nods silently to Uribe.

Uribe takes the laptop and exits the room.

"Rosalie, darling, it's alright now. We are going to stop him. He won't hurt anybody again." Carefully, she pulls Rosalie's face away. Sitting face to face now, Teresa uses her thumbs to wipe Rosalie's tears from her cheeks. "You need to tell me what happened after you crossed the border."

Nodding, Rosalie takes a deep breath and blinks hard several times. "Cucuy took me to a house and they let me out of the truck. It was night, and two men took me to a shed behind a big house. The taller man held a knife to my eye and told me to be quiet all night. To not say a word or he would cut my breasts off."

Teresa removes two pictures from inside her notepad. She shows a picture of Alger's dead body and a mugshot of Rodrigo to Rosalie.

Rosalie gasps when she sees the picture of Alger's dead body. Of all the villains along her journey, he was the only one that didn't violate her. "Yes. It was them."

"Well, you will be happy to know that they were both killed. Alger was killed by thieves in a field, and Rodrigo was killed at the spa."

Suddenly distressed, Rosalie sits up straighter. "Were any of the girls killed?"

Teresa's brow furrows as she stares at Rosalie. "No. Just Alger. Rodrigo was shot but killed later in the spa by a man named Hector."

Rosalie's eyes open wide with wonder that the powerful men in her life could all be dead. "And the man in the room with me killed Hector?"

"Yes," Teresa nods slowly, "he killed Hector and two other men at the spa."

"So, he was a bad man too?" asks Rosalie.

Teresa pauses and contemplates her answer. Looking at the young, damaged girl before her, she says, "Yes. He was a bad man too."

"I thought he was only like the other men in the field."

This brings Teresa up short. "You've been to the field?"

"Yes. The morning after I slept in the shed, they put the eight of us in a van and drove us to a field. They made us lay on rugs for the men."

Teresa grimaces at the thought of this young girl being raped by dozens of men one after another. She can't bring herself to ask any more questions about the sex. "You poor girl. This is not going to happen to you again. Do you have any family left?"

Rosalie looks down at her hands, fidgeting with the blanket again as she fights the urge to cry. "My mother is still in Cochoapa el Grande. The men there told her that she had to work for them now."

"Wait here. I'm going to go talk to my boss and see if we can find your mom. What's her name?"

For the first time since they met, Teresa sees hope in Rosalie's eyes. "María Bolanos."

Teresa stands up and turns to exit the room. As she's about to leave, Rosalie asks, "Do they know that I'm talking to you?"

"Don't worry. You're safe now."

Rosalie pulls the blanket tighter and hopes that she is hearing truth.

Outside, Uribe is speaking on his cell phone when Teresa walks up to him. "Yeah. Jeffrey Floding, two-sixteen Trask Street, Laredo, Texas. Have the local PD pick him up, and notify border patrol in case he tries to flee into Mexico," says Uribe, before he hangs up the phone.

"You're not gonna put surveillance on him and try to catch him in the act?" Teresa asks, surprised.

"Fuck no. No more of this 'letting them slip through our fingers' bullshit. We have enough with Rosalie and Elena describing how he gets them across. I'm sure the other girls will be more open to speak up once they see him in hand cuffs."

"Fine with me. The sooner we get this piece of shit off the streets, the better. I'm gonna call over to the Mexican Consulate and have them try and get in touch with Rosalie's mom," says Teresa as she sits down at her desk.

"Whoa, whoa, whoa. That's for the counselors to do. We need to get on this Cucuy thing. He's all we have on this cell. Both pimps and a spa manager are down. Their handler is also dead. There is a vacuum of leadership here. Without Cucuy, we've got nothing on their next level of management." Exasperated, Uribe shakes his head. "I'm sorry, but two of my agents are dead and I can't have you playing nursemaid to that girl, no matter how sad her story is."

Teresa stares at him indignantly. "Come the fuck on, man! I promised that girl that we would help her."

"And we will. We have other people to take care of that stuff. You're a lawman. You catch bad guys. Your place is on that phone right now, getting all this out for dissemination. You need to start checking on the LLC that owns the spa. You need to go investigate the owner of the house that those girls were held prisoner in. You need to go do your fucking job," Uribe orders as he stands and puts on his jacket.

"So what are you gonna be doing while I'm here doing all this important investigative work?" Teresa retorts, her anger beginning to boil over.

"I'm gonna be standing beside Ulrika as she sees her dead husband's body. We've got two agents in the morgue, and eight sex slaves waiting for hope...GO PROTECT THEM. FIND BAD GUYS," Uribe yells at her with slow, deliberate emphasis on each word.

Teresa folds her arms and glares at her boss, letting the contempt she feels come through plainly on her face.

"Don't give me that look. You know the game. Don't get played. How much of her story is a fabrication?" He gestures toward the interrogation room, oblivious to the fact that Teresa is ready to punch him in the face. With a righteous superiority, he continues, "You know how these girls work. She may have cooked up the part about her dad being murdered to garner sympathy from you. The fact is, she's sixteen; she's getting asylum no matter what. I have no need for her crocodile tears."

Without another word, Uribe exits the office and leaves Teresa alone with her thoughts and her clenched fists. Hating him for it, she knows he has a point; her purpose is what it is. She needs to let go. She needs to believe in the system.

Teresa walks to the locker room and turns the dial on her lock. As she pulls the padlock open, she glances left at the locker next to hers. "G. Granado" is handwritten on the label across the top. Various navy stickers are plastered across the remaining door front. To the right, she sees Bennett's locker. The label across the top reads, "L. Bennett," and underneath, "FNG" is written. Teresa laughs softly to herself as she fights back tears. "Fucking New Guy," she mutters. Flanked by the memory of her fallen comrades, she

ROSALIE'S CROSSING

finds the resolve to let Rosalie go. From inside, she collects a gym bag and closes the locker.

She walks back to the interrogation room and finds young Rosalie sitting as if she hadn't moved a muscle while Teresa was away. "Hey, *chica*. I brought you some of my clothes to change in to."

She unzips the bag and removes a pair of sneakers, along with white socks, gym shorts, a t-shirt, and a sports bra. "No one will see you in here. You can change in to these. Just knock on the door when you are done," says Teresa as she walks to the door and exits back into the office.

Teresa takes a moment to lean against the door and tries to forget about the terrible day. She closes her eyes and tries to picture her friends as they were, but she can't see them laughing in the office, "Busting Balls" or "Smoking and Joking." She can only see Bennett lying in a pool of blood, and Gabriel for what he truly was— a monster. She hears a knock and opens the door.

There stands Rosalie, for the first time in a while, looking as she should. Standing in the slightly oversized clothes, she looks like a kid on her first day of gym class. The running mascara and sad face are the only holdovers from her recent life.

Teresa puts her arm around the exhausted girl and says, "Come on. Let's get you downstairs. They will take care of you down there."

Rosalie knows what's happening. Another promise is being broken. Teresa won't make sure she sees her mom again. Rosalie knows that she is just being passed off to another caretaker—another caretaker that might possibly be kind, but most likely will not care for her at all. The two women walk together, toward the elevator, and wait as they hear the hum of the motor. Rosalie has made peace with her suffering, and she takes the opportunity to tilt her head to the right and rest it against Teresa's arm.

Teresa looks at the young girl in the reflection of the elevator's metal sheen and feels powerless.

CHAPTER SEVENTEEN
ASYLUM

Foreign born victims of sex trafficking have options. Some choose to return to their native country and face the persecution of being a whore. Many choose to receive asylum in the United States. Rosalie's decision isn't an easy one; with her entire soul, she desires to be held by her mother again. One fateful phone call will break her heart forever.

Teresa gives her one last hug and whispers, "Everything will be alright in the end. Good things happen to good people," then hands her a granola bar before giving her over to Melanie Mason.

Ms. Mason is a counselor working for the Department of Immigration and Customs Enforcement. One of her many duties is to process and counsel minors that have fallen victim to the sex trade. In Spanish, she says, "Rosalie, my name is Melanie. I'm going to make sure you are taken care of. I need you to trust me. There are a lot of things that we are going to need to do. OK?"

Rosalie hesitates, looking to Teresa for encouragement, then nods her head.

Teresa smiles sadly. "I have to go now. I've got to go catch the bad guys. Melanie is going to take good care of you."

Rosalie returns the smile half-heartedly, then looks up at Melanie as Teresa walks back to the elevator.

It's early morning and Rosalie hasn't slept in what feels like days. As she follows the woman to her office, Melanie tells her, "I know you're probably tired, sweetheart, but we have a lot that we need to get done. We need to get you over to the hospital to give you a medical examination, but first I have to start your file."

Over the next few hours, Rosalie answers a variety of questions, from her date of birth, to her parents' names, to the number of sexual partners during her time as a sex slave. Rosalie goes through the motions, hoping that a soft bed and a hot meal are in her future. The best she gets is twenty minutes of sleep in the passenger side of an old government vehicle, and a bologna sandwich for breakfast.

At the hospital, she waits in a cold examination room, wearing a paper gown. The doctor enters and Melanie translates everything he says for Rosalie. She learns they will have to swab her vagina and take blood from her arms.

The rapid AIDS test comes back negative. Melanie is excited to relay the news, though Rosalie is unsure what it means. Finally, it's time for the exam. As she lies back on the examination table, spreading her bent knees wide as instructed, she tries to ignore the doctor's cold, gloved hands. Flashes of Rey, Cucuy, Rodrigo, Gabriel, and other faceless men, more than she can count, fill her mind as the doctor inspects her. To fight off the images in her head and the terror that comes with them, she stares at the light in the ceiling, keeping her eyes open wide.

The doctor informs them that she is in the initial stages of a herpes outbreak on her vagina and anus. Thinking she is sick, she begins to cry, and he assuages her fears by explaining what it is and telling her that it's manageable with medication, and to avoid sexual contact during an outbreak. She finds herself thinking that won't be difficult, if they keep their word; she has no interest in sexual contact.

It's nearing midmorning by the time she is back in her gym clothes and on her way back to the ICE field office.

Ms. Mason listens to her voicemail. She has one new message: "Ms. Mason, this is Javier Ortiz, of the Policía Federal. We sent word to the town in question. We forwarded your contact information to the local official, and he will have Mrs. Bolanos contact you as soon as possible. If I can be of further assistance, please don't hesitate to call. *Buenos dias.*"

"Well, it's a start. Hopefully she'll call today, because we can't keep you here long term," Ms. Mason tells Rosalie.

"If you can't find my mother, what will happen to me?"

"Well, since you are under eighteen, you will be handed over to the Texas State Department of Child Services. They will place you in foster care."

Rosalie has never heard of this before, and she fears it might be more of the same. "What does that mean?"

Melanie looks at her with a kind smile. "Fostering is when you go live with a family that agrees to look after you until you become an adult."

"Who? Do I get to pick?"

"No, you will just go to whoever is available. It's not as bad as some people make it out to be."

Rosalie feels that knot in her stomach again. "What if I was eighteen years old now?"

"Well, that's a different story. If you were eighteen, we would just grant you amnesty, and start the process of naturalizing you. You'd become a U.S. citizen eventually. Or, if you wanted, we could repatriate you back to Mexico."

Such a big decision for a child to make. Take the "easy" path and stay in America, or return to her native land?

"Listen, why don't you go over to that couch and take a nap? I have a lot of paperwork to get to. I'll wake you if your mother calls."

This is the best idea she's heard so far, and the easiest decision she's had to make. Rosalie rises from her chair and walks over to the couch. It's a classic government procured couch. Worn from years of use, it has cigarette burns from a time when smoking in a federal facility was the norm. Paranoid that she can still fall victim to misfortune, she lays down on her side, facing out. She rests both hands under her head and uses them as a pillow.

Ms. Mason looks up from her computer to check on the girl, and upon seeing this sad attempt at comfort, decides to put her work on hold and help. "Here, baby," she says, laying an old windbreaker jacket over Rosalie, then opens the bottom drawer of a nearby desk and produces a pillow. "It's old, and hasn't been washed in years, but it's good enough for the overnight guy."

Rosalie breaks from her paranoia for a moment to say thank you and accept the kind gesture. Once her head touches the pillow, she falls fast asleep.

As she sleeps, she dreams of the mountainside farm where she grew up. She sees her father preparing a row of soil for his lettuce crop. He looks up for a moment to smile and wave at her before returning to his work. She turns around toward her home and sees her mother in the doorway. Her mother's beautiful, long hair dances in a gust of wind. The smile on her mother's face is warm and welcoming.

As she runs toward her mother, she feels a drop of rain hit her cheek. She stops to look up toward the sky; there's a dark raincloud overhead. She tries to look back toward her mother but can't. Her head is stuck—she can't move.

She is pulled from her dream into the darkness of reality. As her eyes adjust to the fluorescent light that fills the room, she realizes a hand grips her forehead and pins the back of her head to the pillow. *It's Cucuy!* Her heart races as adrenaline shoots like a bullet through her body. He spreads her legs, beginning to mount her. She can't move; she is powerless.

Just as he leans in to kiss her face, the sound of a ringing telephone jolts her from the nightmare. Now fully awake, she surveys the area. The light from outside isn't as bright; it's almost dusk. Ms. Mason is still at her desk, just as she was when Rosalie fell asleep.

"Ahh, great...she's right here. Give me a moment to get her," she says to the person on the other end of the phone. She holds up the receiver. "Rosalie, it's your mother."

Rosalie can't contain her excitement. Her feet almost slip out from under her as she runs across the floor in her socks. Nearly snatching the phone out of Ms. Mason's grasp, she cries into it, "Mama, I'm so scared! Please, come get me! Please!"

There is nothing but silence on the other end. After a few moments, she can hear increasingly heavy breathing. Then: "Rosalie..."

It's her mother, but something is wrong...she doesn't sound right. "Mama, please, please! Come get me," pleads Rosalie once more.

"Rosalie. You need to stay away! Get far away!" A hollow thud rings out through the phone's speaker as the receiver on her mother's end falls to the ground.

For a moment, there's nothing but muffled static, then someone picks up the telephone and speaks, a man: "We told you what would happen if you ran. *Tu madre* is going to pay for your sins. We're gonna burn her, and feed her to the rats. You say anything else to *la policía*, and we'll do worse to you."

The phone call ends with a click. The phone slides from her hand as she realizes she's alone in the world.

Ms. Mason looks over. "Well, what did she say?"

At first, she can't control the breaths that come rapidly, in and out, as her heart thunders through her small frame, shaking her to the core. Her mother...

Then, she looks up at Ms. Mason, a steely resolve settling within her as she forces the panic down. It's now that Rosalie decides her path. She now has control over her journey. Her first act is to not cooperate with anyone else's idea of her destiny. She knows evil. She knows pain. She knows that if she is to survive, she must adapt. The cartel has a reach that far exceeds its grasp. No one, not even Teresa, can protect her. Not because they don't care, but because they can't care. They have endless casework. New women are brought over the border every minute of the day. New tragedies are happening every second.

Rosalie is not special to them. Rosalie is not special to anyone anymore. She decides, right then and there, that she will no longer be a victim. She thinks of the heroes, and how they are no different than the villains. She stares at Ms. Mason with contempt. She will not help Rosalie, so in turn, Rosalie will now stand mute. She refuses to answer any of the woman's questions. She will go along with the process, but she will not be a slave anymore.

Her real journey has just begun.

THE

END

58188443R00099

Made in the USA
Middletown, DE
05 August 2019